A BEAST
IN PARADISE

Cécile Coulon

A BEAST
IN PARADISE

*Translated from the French
by Tina Kover*

Europa
editions

Europa Editions
1 Penn Plaza, Suite 6282
New York, N.Y. 10019
www.europaeditions.com
info@europaeditions.com

Copyright © 2019 by L'iconoclaste, Paris
First Publication 2021 by Europa Editions

Translated by Tina Kover
Original title: *Une bête au paradis*
Translation copyright © 2021 by Europa Editions

Library of Congress Cataloging in Publication Data is available
ISBN 978-1-60945-647-4

Coulon, Cécile
A Beast in Paradise

Book design by Emanuele Ragnisco
www.mekkanografici.com

Original cover design by Quintin Leeds
Cover image: Istockphoto.com/tbratford

Prepress by Grafica Punto Print – Rome

Printed and bound in Great Britain by Clays Ltd, Elcograf S.p.A.

Her lips touched mine
And I felt a vague burning in my heart.
—JULES SUPERVIELLE, "The Portrait"

On either side of the narrow road snaking through rich green fields, the green of storms and of grass, flowers—enormous, pale-hued, fragile-stemmed flowers—bloom all year round. They run alongside this ribbon of asphalt until it joins up with a path marked by a wooden stake, capped by a sign reading:

YOU HAVE REACHED PARADISE

Below this, the path, pocked with brown puddles, leads into a large yard, a rectangle of beaten earth, weeds nibbling at its slightly rounded corners. The barn is spotless. A tractor and a little blue car are parked in front of it, both regularly washed. On the other side of the yard, chickens, geese, a rooster, and three ducks waddle in and out of a long shed perforated with low openings. The ground here is thickly strewn with golden grain. The henhouse overlooks a steep slope flanked by a brook that dries up each year in the summer heat. On the horizon, the fields of Bas-Champs ripple in the breeze, frogs and herons stirring the dark waters of Sombre-Étang, nestled in its fern-filled hollow.

A centuries-old oak tree stands in the center of the yard, its branches high enough to hang a man or a tire swing, its shade so cool and pervasive that in the autumn, when Blanche comes out of the house to make her daily round of the property, the masses of dead leaves and the deep crimson hue of them make her feel as if she's walking on ground that has been bleeding all night. She passes the chicken coop, the barn, the dog—perhaps the twelfth or thirteenth one she's known here; it has no name, they just call it "Dog," like the others before it—and makes her way quickly to the pigpen, a circle of boards with a swinging door whose latch sticks in the winter cold. The ground is leathery here, packed hard by years of trampling and now abandoned, untouched by feet or hooves.

In the pen itself, so vast for a place no longer sheltering any animals, in the pen Blanche stands straight-backed, despite the eighty years that weigh heavy on her heart, etching deep lines in her face and transforming her fingers into broken twigs.

The pen is empty, but at its center lies a bouquet of the same flowers that line the asphalt ribbon leading to Paradise. Some of them have wilted already; others—like Blanche herself—are on the verge of losing their last traces of color. It's a small, wild bouquet in a large earthen circle. Shoulders swathed in a scarlet cardigan, redder even than the dead leaves beneath the hanging tree, she kneels tremblingly before this little bouquet, like one that a child might gather to mark her first communion, pulling out the brown stems and throwing them aside in a movement that is startlingly quick, almost violent. From the pocket of her red cardigan, redder than the blood of Paradise, she takes a few fresh blossoms, breathing on them very softly before placing them with the others. She stays there, unmoving, before the little wild bouquet, so lovely in the middle of this pen that her grandmother, Émilienne, had dug for her pigs. It was a long time ago. She remembers everything.

Because even though no animals live in this ring of boards and dirt anymore, one beast comes here each morning, to mourn.

Blanche.

Blanche and Alexandre made love for the first time while the pig was being bled in the yard. They'd closed the windows without drawing the curtains. Downstairs, the party was in full swing. The animal shrieked like a torture victim, the neighboring farmers gathered round, the blood forming large dark poppies in the beaten earth. Under the big tree in front of the door, Louis had set up tables covered with cloths embroidered with the initials of the Émard family. Forty people had come for the bloodletting, the little ones watching, wide-eyed. Émilienne, at the head, called out, "Careful now, careful! The blood, save the blood."

Upstairs, Blanche and Alexandre clung together, naked, intertwined, knowing what to do without knowing how to do it, knowing it would be painful without knowing how to make the pain more beautiful. The odor of blood from the yard competed with the scents of Alexandre's skin and Blanche's sex; they didn't smell anything but each other, didn't hear anything but their mingled breaths, filled with both fear and relief at finding themselves alone together, at last.

Alexandre explored the girl with just his hands and his mouth at first. She lay with her head on the big blue pillows, watching him. He gripped her waist, his tongue and fingers sliding down her stomach like mountain climbers thwarted by a slope. Before he buried his lips between Blanche's thighs, he lifted his head, his gaze resting on the dark auburn curls of her pubic hair. Smiling, he nodded toward the leaves of the tall tree out the window and murmured:

"They're the same color."

She gave a nervous little gasp of laughter. Alexandre caressed her gently, the way you calm a jenny about to give birth, and then his face vanished between her legs. Blanche's hands gripped the boy's shoulders, her fingers digging into his skin, keeping him between her thighs.

"Are you okay?"

He held her close, his arm beneath the nape of her neck. Blanche seemed to be asleep against his shoulder, but her eyes were wide open. She didn't seem sad, or angry. Her deep green eyes were simply fixed on the wall across from the bed, and as hard as Alexandre looked, he did see anything but a wall, with a tiny spider in the corner, very thin, almost elegant, weaving a web.

"Blanche? Are you okay?"

A shiver rippled through her body.

"I've felt nicer things," she said, her fingertips playing around her navel.

"Was it that bad?"

Alexandre sat up. He thought he'd been gentle. She hadn't cried out, or sobbed, or asked him to stop. He'd thought he'd managed pretty well; men had told him the first time always hurt, so it was better to do it quickly.

Blanche sat up too. They leaned back stiffly, almost formally, against the pillows, their cheeks creased with the imprint of the sheets. Blanche drew up her knees and wrapped her arms around them. Suddenly she looked like a little girl.

"Does it hurt?"

She looked up at the ceiling. Her lips moved in the indistinct murmur Alexandre had grown used to hearing. Blanche always chose her words carefully before she spoke, arranging them in order so that her sentences would be clear. She did the same thing in French class. But no one ever made fun of her for it; she was Émilienne's granddaughter.

"Last winter, I stepped on an ember that had popped out of the fire, onto the hearth."

Blanche's voice had changed. It wasn't the voice of a young girl in pain anymore, but the voice of a woman explaining the pain she had suffered once.

"It hurts like stepping on an ember," she said.

Then she kissed him quickly, several times, on the nose and the corners of his mouth. Alexandre tried to take her in his arms again, but she pulled away, slipped out of bed, and went to the window.

"The yard'll smell like blood for three days."

The pig's blood permeated everything, its odor suffusing the air of Paradise until the southerly wind drove it away. A thick layer of entrails, excrement, bristly hairs, and dirt coated the fodder. Anywhere you put your hand, your fingers dipped into a pool of hot blood. For three days, or longer if the breeze didn't pick up, Paradise would be covered with the splattered remains of dead animals. Scrubbing and washing were no use; you just had to wait, and eventually the smell would drift away to pervade some other place.

"It never used to bother me, but it makes me nauseous now," grumbled Alexandre, sitting on the bed.

He put his clothes back on very slowly. How long had they been in this room? An hour? More? He had no idea.

Blanche and Alexandre had picked the day and the place for their first time a few weeks earlier. Alexandre's mother was a cleaning lady for both the village school and the local notary; his father, a ticket agent at the train station in the next town over. Their son left the house before they did in the mornings, and came back late in the evening, hours after they'd gotten home. On weekends his parents kept firmly to their living room, and in summers to their postage stamp of a garden, kept up as meticulously as some eighth wonder of the world, at the end of the little dirt path that veered at right angles off the main road. Impossible for two teenagers to be alone there. Likewise, at Paradise, somebody was always around: Émilienne, busy in the kitchen, entertaining in the dining room, asleep upstairs. When she went out "to the animals," Louis, her farmhand, kept a close eye on things to make sure all was in order. Occasionally the two of them were out of the house at the same time, but never for very long. And anyway, Blanche hated it when both of them were gone. Aware that she would inherit the whole place one day, being there alone filled her with anxiety. She was afraid she wouldn't know how to manage it. At sixteen, she still needed to watch Louis and Émilienne at work, to memorize their movements and store up their strength for the day when Paradise would be entirely dependent on her. Whenever her grandmother and the farmhand left the farm the cows would moo at the other end of the Bas-Champs, the snipes on the banks of the pond flapping off across the water, away from Blanche. After the haying, the bales seemed to mock her, lying there motionless on the stubbled ground.

Even though Blanche loved Paradise, it made her feel very small. The ghosts that inhabited the place took up all the room.

It had been her idea to do it on butchering day.

"We'll stay for the beginning, and when everyone's watching the pig die, we'll sneak upstairs. We'll just have to get back before the guests leave."

Alexandre hadn't said anything. It was there, or the barn, or waiting.

They went downstairs, Blanche first. Louis was busy with the pig's carcass. Watching her walk among the farmers, her complexion rosy and fresh, smiling left and right like a Madonna bestowing blessings, the farmhand was suddenly overcome by an unpleasant sensation. He gripped the animal's feet, bound together by a thick rope, watching the girl who, on this day, had not stayed to witness the pig's death, but had slipped away upstairs to melt into the flesh of a man other than him.

PROTECTING

Louis had worked at Paradise since Émilienne lost her daughter Marianne and son-in-law Étienne in a car accident. The grandmother had found herself alone with Blanche and her brother Gabriel. She had needed someone there at the farm. Not for the children; for all the rest of it.

At the time, Louis was skipping school to work on the sly, delaying as much as possible his return to the family home, which was a sort of bungalow on the edge of a pond filled with sludge rather than water. His father beat him regularly. At first, he'd hit him for no reason, simply because he was one of those men who used his fists instead of his mouth and punches instead of words. But gradually he had begun finding excuses to beat him more often and harder. Louis came home too late, he said, or he wasn't trying hard enough in school, or he was hanging around with a bunch of good-for-nothings. Louis had let the dog get out and now they couldn't find it. Louis had let the potatoes get cold, the fire go out. Louis was stupid, and, worst of all, Louis didn't fight back. He allowed himself to be hit. He was quick, and ran and hid. When night fell, he had no choice but to go home, but his father had never calmed down by then. Quite the opposite. His mother watched them, standing against the kitchen sink, shuddering. Every beating suffered by her son was torture for her; she squeezed her eyes shut and gritted her teeth, compelled to remain silent, broken by years of avoidance, of blows, still in the grip of a hideous love for this husband wracked by torments she didn't understand. He transferred his pain to the bodies of others, his wife and his son, his dog and his trees.

When Blanche and Gabriel's parents died, Louis had turned up at the farm and offered to help Émilienne "until things calmed down." The grandmother, with two children underfoot and no one to support her, assigned him all the duties a farm boy should know how to perform and more. For a month, Louis worked himself to the point of exhaustion at Paradise. The hay pitched into the manger, the heavy blow on the stake to drive it straight and true into the ground, the arms waved overhead to herd cattle or slipped gently beneath the calves to inspect their bellies and throats and jaws. The kilometers walked between fields and barn, barn and pond, pond and kitchen. Back home in the evenings, as the red glow of twilight dipped beneath the horizon, the boy sank into sleep like a fly in a glass of milk.

One evening, as Émilienne was putting the children to bed, he tapped on the dining room window. The night was pitch black. Émilienne let him in. Before she could ask what he was doing there so late, Louis swayed forward. His nose was broken, his lips split.

"I didn't know where else to go."

Émilienne didn't say anything. She wrenched the young man's nose back into place, dabbed at his lips, took off his clothes. His legs and back and stomach were covered with purple bruises fading to pale yellow.

"You'll sleep in the parents' room," she breathed.

"Are you sure?"

"You have a better idea?"

Louis gestured toward the barn, lifting his chin. "I can bed down in the hayloft tonight."

"You're either very tired or very stupid," she scoffed, gently.

She pulled him up from the chair into which he had collapsed, bare-chested in his drawers and a pair of dirty socks, his face ravaged by his father's rage, and took him upstairs.

Louis had never seen a bed so big, or a floor so clean, or a quilt so thick. Nothing seemed real. For him, this room belonging to the departed daughter and son-in-law stank unavoidably of death. And yet, when Émilienne helped him to lie down, he felt as if he'd arrived at the end of a long journey. Here in this bedroom of the dead, his life would begin again.

Louis woke up the next day at two o'clock in the afternoon, his nose and mouth and cheeks feeling as if they were being stabbed by enormous needles. His body creaked in protest. He tried to stand but toppled to the floor. Suddenly, he heard hurried steps and the door was flung open to reveal a pair of tiny feet. Blanche, aged five, stood there looking at him, her eyes those of a curious child, but one already familiar with the horrors of the world.

"Why're you on the floor when there's a bed there?" she inquired, gravely.

Louis tried to answer, but the pain was so paralyzing that he couldn't speak. Blanche came closer and took his hand, and a few seconds later, as he was slipping into unconsciousness, strong arms lifted him and put him back in bed, exactly as they had the night before. He smelled Émilienne's clothes, a smell of damp earth mingled with grain, and fell back to sleep until the evening.

At sunset, on the nightstand, a steaming bowl of soup formed little rings of moisture on the wall. Émilienne sat with a spoon in her hand and fed him very gently. After she had finished and tucked the quilt around him again, she said in a firm voice:

"As of today, you live here. We'll talk when you're feeling better."

Louis made a strange gesture, like an injured monk, dipping his first and middle fingers toward her like a benediction, and drifted to sleep again.

The young man never set foot in the family bungalow again. His mother came to Paradise, just once. Guardedly, Émilienne invited her into the kitchen, served coffee and madeleines, then called Louis. When he spotted his mother through the window, he froze.

"Your father isn't here," Émilienne said, rising to open the door for him. "Come on. She's brought some clothes for you."

As she left, his mother tried to embrace him. He pushed her away.

"Louis is working here. He won't be coming back to live with you, unless he wants to."

The old woman spoke bluntly, in the firm voice of those who refuse to yield in the slightest to the violence of others.

"I was the one who looked after your son that terrible night."

The disgraced mother choked back a sob.

"I'm sorry."

"Apologizing is the very least you can do," Émilienne replied.

She stood up, squeezed the boy's shoulder, and left the room. Louis wanted to follow her, but she turned and gestured for him to stay, the way she would have ordered a dog to sit down in front of the fireplace. The mother looked at her son, whose mouth and nose were still faintly discolored.

"Why don't you leave?" he asked, scratching at the table-cloth with a fingernail. "He'll kill you."

His mother sighed.

"Of course he won't."

She said it with certainty, and Louis heard it in her tone: she loved her husband, despite all she had suffered at his hands. She loved this man the same way an animal worships the master that beats it each morning and strokes it at night. He stood now, as Émilienne had, and left the room, squeezing his mother's shoulder once, like the old woman had squeezed his.

In front of the house, Blanche and Gabriel were playing with the hens. Louis went to the barn, rolled up the sleeves of his coveralls, and began raking the ground in the half-light, without sparing a glance or even a tear for the mother he now allowed to walk away.

Louis was a poor worker at first. Even simple tasks eluded him. The cows crowded back against the fence when he went into the paddock or refused to enter the milking parlor in the morning. The hens taunted him; the rooster chased him while he hopped fearfully around the yard, dodging the thrusts of its sharp beak. Émilienne had forbidden him from being violent with the animals, so he ran from them, or tried to befriend the uncooperative ones. He looked like an idiot. It took him six months to herd the cows without any of them escaping, for the rooster to scurry out of the way when he approached, for his muscles to develop. He was sixteen years old.

In a matter of months, Émilienne turned him into a useful man. She taught him to fence fields, to recognize and cut down ash, pine, and chestnut trees; he memorized the names of the meadow plants, the grasses, and the wild stock. He learned that the cows loved alfalfa and clover, but that the tiny blue flowers bloated their bellies. Then came the slaughtering of the pigs, the skinning of rabbits, the sluicing of the henhouse. He squeezed the cows' udders in the rhythm dictated by Émilienne. "Milking an animal should be like keeping time with a song," she said. He assisted with the birthing of two calves. The first time, the veterinarian showed him where to position himself, how to help the mother; the second time Émilienne woke him before dawn, saying it was time for his final "practical exam." He managed well, flushed with sweat and anxiety, exhausted alongside the little calf, its mother licking its warm muzzle, the hair sticky with blood.

The pigpen was the only place he had felt comfortable right

away. The very first time he ventured into the enclosure, the animals had surrounded him curiously, snuffling benignly at his coveralls. Scratching at the earth with their hooves, grunting happily, they fell upon the scraps Louis piled in the corner of the pen, here at the southern tip of Paradise.

During those first days, after his forced rest, Émilienne had asked Louis to be there when she killed a chicken for lunch or skinned a rabbit. Louis watched carefully, memorizing each movement; the blow to the hen's head and then the quick twisting of its neck; the rolling back with the fingertips of the rabbit's skin as it hung head-down from a nail on the wall; the feathers plucked out one by one, the entrails tossed into a pan for the pigs. He watched Émilienne the way a cat eyes a bird through a closed window. Her contours molded by an endless series of deaths, she looked up at him, green eyes glimmering, radiating that strength, that gentleness, that were such an integral part of her. At last, one day, she gazed at him for a long time, hands slippery with the guts of the chicken just beheaded on an old newspaper in the kitchen, and said, with a real smile—not a half-smile, not a smirk, but a real one, wide and deep and open:

"Your place is here now."

BUILDING

L ouis slept in Marianne and Étienne's bed until Blanche and Gabriel stopped sharing a room. The brother and sister had the bedroom at the top of the stairs, but on Blanche's eleventh birthday, Émilienne decided that the girl would sleep in her mother's bed from now on, alone. Louis was dispatched to Gabriel's room, to a narrow mattress next to the boy's bed.

When you went down the dirt road with the sign reading YOU HAVE REACHED PARADISE, you ended up in the yard, lined with farm buildings, a fortress of wooden planks humming with insects and smelling of cow dung and straw and animal hair. At its center, during the summers, the tree provided a spreading canopy for the child-sized table and benches snugged against its trunk. The house rose up to the right of the path, built of dark stone, its windows overlooking the Bas-Champs. In the distance lay Sombre-Étang and its dark-plumed occupants, the sky clear and violet-hued on the horizon. The henhouse perched on the edge of a sudden, steep slope that ran down into the woods where Émilienne gathered twigs for the fire. A footbridge spanned the small brook and led to several hectares of meticulously maintained fields planted with rye grasses, sweet vernal grasses, foxtail. Woodland ringed the landscape to the east, a dark and leafy belly from which flocks of powerful-winged birds would erupt. Louis knew every inch of Paradise now. The farm had once belonged to Émilienne's husband, a simple and hard-working man killed by lung disease. On his death, the land had passed to his wife and daughter, Marianne—who had left Paradise at eighteen, lured by the siren song of the city.

Five years later, Marianne had returned, now engaged to a young geography student she'd met on the green lawns of the university. Étienne was a gentle young man, not very tall and rather thin. Even the smallest details of the country landscape were enough to send him into raptures.

Émilienne had been wary at first. Marianne seemed so fragile, so incapable of farm work. And her little boyfriend, a hothouse flower, with a complexion as pale as his eyes, and the tangle of hair he never combed, and his voice, softer than a girl's! Étienne had studied, been active in a couple of left-wing groups at the university, then taught for a few months before admitting that he didn't have what it took to handle the rigors of "the real world." He wanted to find a place that would suit him, where he wouldn't feel overwhelmed by anything more than the fatigue of labor well done. Étienne was like one of those city dwellers forever yearning for a sort of untamed utopia, a return to the kind of world they'd only read about in books. For him, Paradise was Robinson Crusoe's island. But when he arrived, Émilienne had nailed him with a piercing stare. He wasn't the type of son-in-law she wanted around— unless he was prepared to work.

Like Louis, he had to learn everything. But unlike Louis, he never managed to reconcile himself to the difficult, repetitive tasks so necessary to daily life on the farm. The only animals he had experience with were his parents' cats, and whenever he set foot in the stable he felt useless, utterly useless faced with these great beasts that could so easily crush him, kill him, and were content simply to stand in their stalls or the pasture and gaze at him with their big, dark-lashed eyes, ears pricked, ruminating on their disdain.

After a few months, Étienne offered his services to the village hall. He could teach private lessons, oversee study halls, tutor struggling students. Anything but the farm. They hired him for fifteen hours a week, to assist the children after school, from five o'clock to eight o'clock in the evening. He was their teacher, their confidant, their supervisor. They gave him a set of keys to the municipal buildings, which he dropped through the hall's mail slot every evening before returning to Paradise, sometimes by car if some good Samaritan stopped to pick him up along the way. He offered to sell the eggs from his mother-in-law's chicken coop himself and deliver them after work to customers who usually drove out to the farm. This meant that Émilienne, without him having to ask, let him use her car. Now Étienne had both the luxury of making the eight-kilometer round trip to town each day by car rather than on foot, and the strange pride of finally being something to Émilienne other than simply an agreeable boy.

Marianne worked alongside her mother, helping with the duties Émilienne would otherwise carry out alone. They spoke little; Émilienne was a woman typical of the region, with no taste for small talk. Her mere presence filled up the space. Marianne was chattier, more lighthearted. She believed in the future, in progress; she was overflowing with ideas for the farm, for making Paradise into an actual paradise. When she'd nailed that wooden sign to the stake at the entrance to the property, Émilienne had laughed, thinking, *She'll get over these whims of hers, these fancies. She'll get over it eventually.* Sometimes the young couple treated themselves to an evening out, dinner at a restaurant, but Émilienne stayed with her animals. She was part of the herd, even though she walked at the front of it.

Blanche and Gabriel were born two years apart. The house quickly filled to bursting with shouts, sobs, laughter, the sound of running feet. The little ones crawled back and forth behind the railing that ran in front of the three bedrooms. At the end of the upstairs hallway, a trap door led to the attic, inhabited by spiders, old furniture, and the dead grandfather's hunting rifle.

Étienne and Marianne made an odd couple. She was as lively as he was dreamy; he was as brilliant as she was impatient. Étienne could guide students through thickets of mathematical problems, grammatical traps, and illustrations depicting the history of France. The structures he built were in the heads of those he taught; his were empires of intellect, castles of the mind. Étienne was "not much for cows," as Émilienne said, but people trusted him, so firmly entrenched did he seem in a world of dates and images, figures and proper nouns.

Marianne had inherited her mother's solid common sense; she brooked no resistance, not even from her two children. Blanche, from earliest infancy, had shown herself to be extremely resourceful. She learned to walk before she could talk, overflowing with movement, as if an older child were hidden inside her, waiting for the right moment to blossom. Even before she started walking, she would crawl the floor until she collapsed, exhausted, at the foot of the staircase, to be scooped up by her mother or grandmother. At age three, Blanche spoke little and walked fast; clever with her hands, she imitated her grandmother's movements. The happiest times were the ones spent with her, frolicking among the hens, sliding between the cows' hooves, taunting the pigs from her perch on the gate of their pen, squashing her nose into a snout with her palm.

Gabriel, on the other hand, was reluctant to do anything. Eat, sleep, walk. He wasn't a difficult child, exactly, but everything seemed to affect him more strongly than it did his sister. The buzzing of a fly woke him up. When Marianne took him outside, the sunlight blinded him, and he screamed. When Émilienne held him, he fell asleep wedged in her armpit. He sat quietly while she balanced him on one hip, tending to her duties. He had been born prematurely, frailer than his sister was at the same age, and more talkative too; the smallest thing set him nattering away. And he was often ill. Mild fevers that lasted a single night, bumpy rashes that came and went, coughing fits, despite his young age and his birth into a family for whom strength wasn't an option but a necessity.

"Life will never be simple for him," murmured Émilienne to Marianne, as the little boy dozed against her shoulder.

His mother sighed.

"You can't tell anything yet; he's too little."

"Can't let melancholy set in, you know. It makes for a poor bedfellow."

Gabriel slept in his parents' room until his first birthday, when he joined his sister at the other end of the hall, in the second bed, the one she'd used when she was that age.

L ittle by little, Louis came to know the Émard family: its absent members, its dead ones, its silent ones. He never asked questions; never pried.

Occasionally, after dinner or at breakfast, the grandmother let a few words slip, or mentioned something about the deceased. Étienne "always looked like he'd just gotten out of bed;" Marianne "didn't talk much, but she was so pretty." She showed him photos of her daughter from before she'd left Paradise for the city. Louis thought Gabriel had inherited his father's quality of always seeming to be a little bit somewhere else, his delicate physique and his slightly dry air, calm no matter what the circumstance.

But Blanche, Blanche could have been Émilienne's daughter, rather than her granddaughter; her movements, the way she held herself, her expressions—all were her grandmother's. Having realized very early that her parents' presence would fade rapidly from Paradise and that another behavioral model would become key to her survival, Blanche had turned to Émilienne, had opened her heart wide, to learn everything that this woman who was as respected as a priest, or a witch, could teach her. Louis understood this even when Blanche was still a child. At night, she would sleep curled up in front of her grandmother's door, Gabriel awakening in their bedroom alone.

Sometimes, as he watched her grow up, Louis wondered if Blanche remembered that she had had parents once, that they had died one stormy evening on the hill people called The Pin. Émilienne's car had flipped coming around a sharp bend in the road, killing them both instantly. The car had been found ten yards down the slope, lying on its side, and the bodies of Marianne and Étienne, as bloody as the day they were born, pulled from the wreckage beneath a nightmarish fall of rain. Blanche knew all that. Very naturally, the little girl became her grandmother's shadow, casting aside her grief in favor of Émilienne's robust self-discipline. It was as if Émilienne alone could extract her from this hell, this sudden absence she had sensed coming, the way a dog can sniff out a storm hours before the first lightning bolt strikes.

It took Gabriel a long time, too long, to understand that his parents were not coming back. At three years old, he shied away from death, hoping it was only temporary, asking Émilienne, Blanche, Louis, anyone who came in the door, nearly every day, if Papa and Mama were "late," if Papa and Mama would "come tomorrow." Blanche just shook her head, avoiding his questioning gaze, while Louis took the little boy on his knee, distracting him by showing the colorful pictures in the books Étienne himself had written and drawn for his children. Émilienne always answered his questions with a simple "no," each time he asked them, "no." The more she said it, the more Gabriel raised his voice, refusing to accept defeat, until one evening in front of the fireplace he climbed into his grandmother's lap and screamed, "Is Papa here? Is Mama here?" He was crying, fat tears rolling down his cheeks. Émilienne gripped his hands so he wouldn't lose his balance, and when he began kicking at her legs with his little feet she grasped him by the waist and said, too loudly to be drowned out by her grandson's snuffling sobs:

"They aren't here anymore. They aren't coming back."

Gabriel opened his mouth. Émilienne pressed her long-fingered hand to his lips. Louis watched the scene from the table where he sat, peeling an orange. He had never seen the toddler so worked up; he had never seen the old woman so angry.

"If you want to cry, do it outside."

She took her hand away and Gabriel screamed even louder than before. Émilienne got up and took him out to the front porch, then stepped back inside, closing the door behind her, leaving the boy outside. Louis could hear him hammering on the door with his fists and screaming, screaming, screaming; even Louis's own father, during his fits of rage—God knew they seemed endless—had never shouted so loudly. It was as if the child's internal organs were going to come flying out of his mouth, so angrily, so violently was he bawling. Louis would never have imagined a four-year-old body capable of making such an earsplitting noise.

"Let him back in, Émilienne."

"No. He has to get it all out," she said, sitting down in front of the fire again.

"What if he runs away?" he asked, rising to go and open the door.

Émilienne gestured for him to sit back down.

"He's not going anywhere. He's a four-year-old boy, not a dog."

She stared into the flames dancing on the hearth, deaf to her grandson's cries.

"Please, let him in," Louis begged.

But the grandmother seemed hypnotized by the fire; there was nothing to be done. Louis stood up, put his dirty plate in the sink, brushed the crumbs off the tablecloth with his hand, and tossed them into the fireplace.

"I'm going to bed."

"Good night. Don't even think about opening that door."

He stalked out of the room, Gabriel's screams echoing in his head.

The child eventually calmed down. Once silence had fallen, Émilienne waited another half an hour. When she opened the door, Gabriel was sitting on the porch steps. Surprised, she moved toward him, thinking he might have exhausted himself and fallen asleep, but no; he was just sitting there, his back very straight. His grandmother sat down next to him and ran her hand through his hair, wide-palmed and large. Her palm stroked Gabriel's head and he melted into her almost instantly. Before carrying him up to his bedroom, where Blanche snored indifferently, her face turned toward the wall, Émilienne let her gaze sweep the farm, the barn swathed in darkness, the boughs of the oak tree drooping over the yard, bowed by the deaths of Marianne and Étienne while the house continued to live. For an instant, Émilienne saw her daughter there, lounging with her back propped against the tree, and tears rose thickly in her throat, tears she gulped back down before they could reach her eyes, which always remained dry. Then, very gently, so as not to wake Gabriel, she stood up on legs made thin and wiry by hard work, by comings and goings, by the bearing of children and of coffins, and let herself be swallowed up by the house, leaving the tree to weep in her stead, turning her attention to the living sleep of Blanche and Louis. That sleep, in this house, here, deep in Paradise—Émilienne was proud of it. Prouder of it than she was of the place itself, because she had raised these young ones up out of the grief and misery in which they'd been mired; Louis, crushed by his father's fists, and Blanche and Gabriel, crushed by their parents' deaths.

When it struck Louis that Blanche wasn't a little girl anymore, he closed himself off, full of shame, of a feeling of violence that reminded him of his father's. It wasn't that he wanted to raise a hand to Blanche; on the contrary, the hand that pounded wooden stakes into the moist earth of Paradise, that drove the cows to pasture—he wanted it to tangle gently in Blanche's hair, to brush it against the nape of her neck, covering it softly the way the eiderdown quilt had covered his wounds, years ago. Watching her transform before his eyes, Louis understood why Émilienne had given her the big bedroom all to herself.

Since they met, Louis and Blanche had treated each other like cats occupying the same territory, polite but distant. Émilienne had never seen the young man as a third grandchild; she always said two was quite enough. Whenever she thought about her farmhand's father, she wondered how the man, who she'd known before he became such a terror, had reached a point where he lashed out at anyone within reach. Louis never spoke about his parents. His mother's sole visit had left a gaping emptiness inside him. He had not seen his father since the night he fled, bleeding, to Paradise. The older man hadn't dared to come to Émilienne's home; he considered it an evil place. Cursed by the sudden death of Émilienne's husband. Cursed by the accident that had taken Marianne and Étienne and orphaned two children at such a young age, leaving them here on these harsh plains, amid these forests forever trying to devour the landscape and the men who lived there. Paradise was a cursed place, run by an angel with cheeks as hollow as a tin pail, her shoulders slightly stooped, her bosom too large for her compact frame.

Émilienne looked like what the land had made of her: a sturdy tree with twisted branches. Her hands, her feet, her ears seemed to sprout from her torso, while her legs and hips and midriff were gnarled, almost nonexistent, nothing but muscle and bone. Émilienne was solid but broken; she had picked up the pieces of her own life, rising each morning at dawn and going to bed at night after Gabriel, Blanche, and Louis were already asleep, knowing that one of them would have to take over for her one day. To hold Paradise together the way you gather a litter of kittens into a damp towel. The sole focus of her existence was this place and the lives lived within it. Everything began and ended with her.

After her husband's death, people had murmured in the village that Émilienne had suffered more than most, that this suffering had given her added substance. After all, garbage nourished pigs and made them stronger. The repeated sorrows had given her a sort of power, a fortitude that grew ever mightier in the imaginations of those who interacted with her. Émilienne had always been an old woman. Not an elderly lady; an old woman. The kind that continue, relentlessly, to consolidate their small empires through the sheer strength of their spirits, which are so immense, so densely peopled with miracles and horrors, so monumental.

Louis had respected her before he loved her, with the kind of love that isn't spoken or shown. A little boy's love.

With Blanche, it was different. The difference in their ages; the closeness and strangeness of the ties that bound them, made them into unexpected companions. They were on the same path. Louis's parents were still alive; sometimes in the night, the idea of going to the bungalow crossed his mind, but then he remembered five-year-old Blanche coming into his room, more curious than surprised; he remembered the little girl who had lost both of her parents at the same time, clinging to Paradise like a ravenous squirrel. Blanche was walking next to him or he next to her. Despite being so much older, despite having lived alongside her every day for nearly eight years, he still felt beaten sometimes, disjointed, crushed beneath the gaze of this young girl whom tragedy had strengthened instead of destroying. Louis would have loved to have Blanche for a sister. He would have protected her, loved her, undoubtedly grumbled a bit at her too, but their relationship would have been clear. He would have understood its limits, the lines that couldn't be crossed, the pools into which boys weren't to dip their toes. But instead he simply coexisted with her, not knowing what to say in her presence, or what to do to amuse her, or draw her attention.

The summer she was thirteen, Blanche had come up the hill from the henhouse and joined her grandmother beneath the willow tree. She'd been catching the little frogs that filled the brook, knocking them hard against a stone, to be grilled on the front porch that evening beneath Émilienne's watchful eye. She found the old woman in her usual spot. The mid-afternoon heat hung thick in the air; Blanche wore a cutoff pair of her father's old trousers, her thin legs like two Q-tips stuck in the ground. A baggy, sleeveless light-gray shirt half-tucked into her shorts hung down over her nonexistent hips, accentuating the paleness of her skin. When she came to stand next to Émilienne, the two of them looked like figures in an old paint-ing, frozen in the dazzling summer light. The same green eyes, the same white skin, the same dark hair. Louis was in front of the barn, smoking a cigarette.

Blanche showed her thigh to Émilienne, who bent over her granddaughter's leg.

"It's a tick."

Émilienne motioned to Louis. "Go and get me some vinegar. And be careful with your cigarette. If that catches fire"—she gestured to the barn—"you'll be the first to burn."

Louis obeyed. He ran to the kitchen, putting out his cigarette by running the butt under cold water, and hurried back, the bottle in one hand and a pair of tweezers in the other.

"You thought of everything," said Blanche, laughing.

"That's my job, isn't it?" Louis retorted.

Émilienne poured a few drops into her hand and shoved the cuff of Blanche's shorts up her thigh. Louis was hit by the smell of vinegar in the heat. Blanche's bare foot, resting in Émilienne's lap, seemed like nothing but a clumsy arrangement of bones. Her ankle stuck out like a hinge, the tracery of veins clearly visible beneath the white skin, the whole leg up to her thigh mottled with darker spots, like raisins in cake batter.

He had never seen Blanche's body so close up, positioned so that the curve of her buttock swelled like a little hill just above Émilienne's hand. Louis imagined the texture of her skin beneath his rough hands, imagined what he would do if he were in Émilienne's place, and a bolt of jealousy, as surprising as it was violent, shot through him. He resented Émilienne for having that body in her hands. The girl was watching her grandmother remove the parasite from her thigh, but something—instinct, surely—made her look up, and when she noticed Louis a few meters away, his gaze riveted to her leg, she nearly yanked her foot off Émilienne's lap. But she stopped herself and stared defiantly back at the farmhand, who vanished, trembling, into the trees in the direction of the pigpen.

"Don't be angry at him," murmured Émilienne, pulling out the tick with a single twisting motion. "He won't hurt you."

"What if I hurt him?"

Émilienne patted her foot. "Don't toy with him. Go and put away the vinegar."

Blanche grabbed the bottle, her heels thumping on the porch steps. The house was cool, and a shiver ran through her. As she washed the tweezers in the sink, she let the cold water run over her fingers, wondering if a boy's touch would be like this, refreshing on a hot summer's day.

L ouis became strange.
     Blanche began locking the bathroom door and avoiding the barn when he was working in it. At mealtimes, she took Gabriel's place, sitting next to him, never across from him. From the head of the table, Émilienne watched Blanche growing up. Her granddaughter was finally realizing that Louis, at twenty-three, was neither her brother nor simply an employee. Perhaps desire would get the best of Blanche one day, propelling her into Louis's arms. Émilienne had considered the possibility. They would make a handsome couple, she thought, but the girl had met him too early. He wasn't a family member, or a friend. Louis held no charm for the Émards' daughter, no erotic power; he was like a household pet, intelligent and docile. She loved him in that way, but that was all. Gradually registering the effect her young body was having on him, Blanche patiently set traps along the path that led to her—but Louis never fell into them. It wasn't that he was ashamed by his reaction; he was embarrassed, yes, embarrassed that she had caught on so quickly, had known even before he had, maybe, anticipating his movements and his looks to the point of locking herself away, in a single afternoon. Louis refused to believe that he had become that sort of man, too invested in the land, too close to Émilienne to upset her equilibrium. But there it was: he had looked at Blanche.

     Blanche was always watching, planning each move before her opponent could make his. She was angry at Louis: through his eyes she had become aware of her own transformation.

Very early on, her grandmother had explained to her that women's bodies were "cities" and men's bodies were "villages." Women's forms were constantly changing, evolving, blossoming beneath the gazes of others, their surfaces filling out in some places and curving inward in others. Men's bodies, on the other hand, once adolescence had passed, kept the same size and appearance. Age and alcohol might cause them to soften and bulge, but they did not transform. Blanche would have to prepare herself for great changes, her grandmother had said. Her little city would become larger, fuller, more desirable. Louis was no predatory raptor circling the carcass of childhood, but still, as she sat next to him and he kept his eyes fixed on his plate, Blanche had to stop herself from slapping him, screaming at him that it wasn't her fault that her buttocks had grown round. She tugged on her T-shirt, flattening the curves of her breasts, raking her sun-bleached hair across her face like a curtain. She tried to make herself invisible, and despite her rage, she resolved not to be nasty to Louis. Years ago, she had learned, in the worst possible way, how her own anger could backfire on her. She had only been eight years old.

On that day, Blanche had gone upstairs for something and was just on her way back down when her brother, usually so calm, burst out of his room with a piece of paper in his hand. In trying to push past her on the staircase he had bumped her ankle and she'd tumbled head-over-heels the rest of the way down. Landing in a heap, it had taken her a moment to untangle her limbs. Her elbows and knees were skinned and scraped. Gabriel had frozen at the top of the stairs watching his sister fall, wide-eyed at the spectacle he had accidentally caused, holding the piece of paper in front of his mouth, and when Blanche had recovered herself somewhat, she ordered him to come down.

Gabriel took a step back. His sister, tense, hunched, lips trembling, gestured with her hand and repeated:

"Get down here. Now."

Gabriel sighed and started down with dragging steps, the stairs creaking beneath his feet. He now held the piece of paper pressed to one thigh, his eyes locked on his sister's. She stood motionless. For a brief moment, he imagined that an enormous dog was poised there, waiting for him, that there was no way to edge past before it leapt on him.

"I didn't do it on purpose, Blanche, I swear."

She sniffed. Gabriel thought she was going to spit on the floor, but she only breathed heavily in and out. He wasn't moving quickly enough for her, and his slowness only made her angrier; her cheeks, already pinkened by fear and the abrasive wood of the stairs, grew even more flushed.

As soon as he set foot on the rug his sister grabbed his arm, the drawing still hanging limply from his hand. With shocking violence, she slapped him with all her strength near the corner of his eye, putting the whole weight of her body into the blow. Just as she lifted her arm to backhand him on the other temple, Émilienne came out of the dining room.

"What's going on here?"

She took in Blanche's bloody elbows, her furious face, the fingers gripping Gabriel's arm. The boy was weeping soundlessly so as not to anger his sister any further; her free hand, still suspended above his head, seemed disproportionately large and heavy.

"Let him go."

Émilienne set her basket down in the doorway. Blanche let go of her brother's arm and he fled into the kitchen.

"Come outside," the old lady grunted, seizing Blanche by the back of the neck as if she were a dog who had shit on the floor.

She took her out to the front porch and pointed to the henhouse.

"Go and fetch Louloute."

She released Blanche, who grasped her grandmother's hand.

"He pushed me on the stairs, and I was angry."

"Go and fetch Louloute, I said."

Tears filled Blanche's eyes. She knew her grandmother; begging would only delay the moment when she, Blanche, would suffer even more than she had in falling down the stairs.

Hanging her head, resigned, she headed toward the slope where a fat brown hen was busily pecking the ground. The chicken, accustomed to the girl's caresses, allowed itself to be picked up. Each of the children had a favorite chicken. Louloute, with her feathers smelling of mud and manure, was Blanche's. As the child was returning to where Émilienne stood waiting, she whispered to Louloute:

"I'm sorry. Gabriel pushed me on the stairs. I'm sorry."

The chicken struggled to get away, but Blanche clutched her more tightly. Reaching the porch, she looked beseechingly at her grandmother one last time. The old lady ignored her, seized the bird by its head, and broke its neck with a twist. The little girl gave a strangled cry. Something in her died at the same moment. She wanted to fling herself on the ground, to weep over this broken heap of feathers, but Émilienne took her by the shoulders before she could move, looking directly into her eyes, murmuring:

"Don't you ever hit your brother again. Do you hear me? Never again."

Blanche hated Émilienne right then.

"Never hurt anyone smaller than you. Never. Or you'll suffer much, much worse in return."

Then she left the girl to her dead chicken.

In the dining room, Louis had heard everything. He was struck by Émilienne's cruelty. At the sound of bone snapping he had, for a few seconds, imagined himself in Blanche's place, trying to absorb some of her pain, her grief, for the animal that had been sacrificed for a lesson he thought foolish and misguided.

Crossing the room, Émilienne paused in front of the fireplace.

"Go with Blanche to bury the chicken."

Louis got up, measuring his words, weighing each gesture, and ventured:

"That might not have been necessary."

Silence. Eyes burning, Émilienne jabbed at a log with the poker.

"Nothing good happens when one person hits another," she said without turning around, "as you should know better than anyone."

Then, without another word, quickly, abruptly, she dismissed him.

Huddled over the body of the chicken, the little girl buried her hands in its feathers, muttering hateful words. Louis couldn't tell whom they were directed at: Émilienne, Gabriel; her parents, maybe? He didn't know, but he had never seen Blanche like this, wholly given over to grief, her childhood lying in pieces around her.

"We'll bury her," he murmured.

Blanche stood up suddenly, annoyed by Louis's presence. When she looked toward the house, she saw Gabriel. He froze, not daring to take another step, and set the piece of paper down on the front porch. Louis went and picked it up; it was damp with tears, and he recognized the tree and the yard, drawn in black pencil. Gabriel had drawn the view from his bedroom and, just beneath the bench, which his childish hand had depicted as being much wider than the trunk against which it leaned, he had written: "For Blanche." Louis held the drawing out to the little girl, whose eyes widened with shock at seeing her name in the misshapen letters of a hand still learning to write. Cradling the dead bird in her arms, she took the paper in her fingertips and walked ahead of Louis over the footbridge leading to the henhouse. There, she asked him to dig a grave like the ones made for humans, and in this gaping hole she wanted to place both Louloute and her brother's drawing. Louis dug a small, circular pit just slightly bigger than the chicken and knelt to place the body in it himself. But Blanche stepped forward, dropping to her knees the way you would next to a brook, and laid Louloute in her final resting place. She ran her fingers gently through the feathers, smoothing them, and then nestled Gabriel's drawing between them.

"He didn't do it on purpose," she whispered, turning to Louis.

The young man nodded. He wanted to say something about Émilienne too, something nasty and scathing, but he bit back the impulse, the old lady's words echoing in his ears.

They went back up to Paradise in silence, Louis walking ahead of Blanche. Halfway up the hill, he held out his hand to help her climb more quickly, but she ignored the gesture and overtook him, suddenly emboldened, resolute. Louis understood, then, that death was a family matter here; that you managed it as a matter of course, the way you fold away a clean sheet.

Alexandre lived in a sterile, soulless little house in the middle of a lonely road narrower than a street, lined with homes crammed closely together. His father worked forty kilometers away as a ticket agent at a railway station. His mother, a cleaner at the town hall, dropped her husband off at work each morning and picked him up in the evening, driving a hundred and sixty kilometers every day, both before and after scrubbing public buildings beneath the eyes of patrons who casually sidestepped the hunched figure bent over the overly broad, glaringly white staircases of the mayor's offices. They filed past this body that might almost have been kneeling in prayer, their eyes lingering without shame on what had, before her marriage, been a superb backside, rounded and firm; the kind of bottom you don't see in the movies, only in real life.

His parents had always been worn out; his mother by work and the never-ending daily drives, his father by boredom, and the frustration of being able to provide nothing for his family but the house. The only unexpected thing in their lives was that they had brought such a beautiful boy into the world. From whom Alexandre had inherited his large eyes and high cheekbones, they had no idea. The more people gushed about his looks, the more confidence he gained. Alexandre did not sink into the melancholy that had stricken his parents at an early age. He grew up thinking that nothing could be worse than the endless silences, the evenings whose agonizing quiet was broken only by the rumble of cars passing the front door. His room, at the end of the hallway next to the bathroom, overlooked the meadow behind the house, which didn't even belong to his parents; a green expanse where cows chewed at the grass, swishing their tails at this boy who had only one desire: to duck under their heavy, rounded bellies and climb onto their broad, comfortable backs, to gain a bit of height, to get some perspective.

He never went through the meadow. The life of this family stopped at his bedroom wall. Alexandre grew up thinking that whatever his future held would be better than this house and these silences. He grew up thinking that maybe, if he worked hard, earned a good living, he would buy this meadow; then his parents would fill it with tables, chairs, animals, games. His father would finally permit himself a smile; his mother would sigh with something other than resignation. A sort of fanatical optimism had taken hold of him very early. Emboldened by so much praise for his physical appearance, Alexandre saw himself as everyone's favorite, certain that this part of his life wouldn't last a moment beyond his youth. He was impatient for it to be over, anxious to show them, all of them, what he was capable of.

The one and only time he remembered his parents discussing anything at the dinner table was from when Alexandre was five years old. It was all anyone in the village could talk about. The car driven by Blanche Émard's parents had flipped on The Pin in a storm. Émilienne was left to raise their two children alone. That evening, Alexandre's parents had envisaged all the possible scenarios. How would the grandmother manage both the farm and the children at her age? Would she send the little ones to live with some distant relatives? Alexandre watched as his mother and father were buffeted by waves of words, torrents of phrases, for the first and last time. The dreadful fate of Marianne and Étienne had woken a passion in them, as sudden as it was fragile. Something had occurred in the life of a person they knew from a distance, something dreadful, insurmountable. Thinking about the Émard family's tragedy made them feel less poor, less crass, less like the ones who would always finish last. A grandmother and her two grandchildren now found themselves in a situation worse than their own, and now they could, from the height of the miniscule step they had just ascended, imagine what would happen next, like schoolmasters leaning over a student struggling with an unsolvable equation.

It was the only thing that occupied them for some time. But they had never offered to help; not even once. People said Gabriel was sad, his head constantly in the clouds. They said Blanche was angry and insolent. They said Émilienne was completely overwhelmed by what had happened. The whole village was busy spinning fantastic stories about the old lady. Alexandre wondered who the Émards were, to arouse so much ardor in his little house, normally so calm. He had met Blanche the way you do a movie star or the heroine of a popular song: through the voices of others. And he had loved her for the life that had, if only just for a brief while, penetrated the walls of his home.

Alexandre realized very quickly that his parents would always be the sort of people whose names you don't remember; the kind referred to as "the ones who have that little house; yes, but which one, the third one down with the meadow behind it, but the meadow doesn't belong to them, such a shame." Once Gabriel and Blanche had gone back to school and Louis was permanently installed in Paradise, silence returned to the dinner table. The hundred and sixty kilometers driven each day were once again marked by stultifying, wordless boredom, fingers clenched on the steering wheel, vacant gazes out the window at fields and forests fuller and richer than the existence of the people contemplating them. Émilienne was stronger, more durable, than they would ever be.

Life resumed its course; Alexandre hurried to grow up, smiling for no reason at everyone, always polite, his demeanor appealing despite being slightly overblown. Outside the house, the boy was talkative. His face changed the moment he stepped beyond the garden gate, the mask of boredom and resignation he wore around his parents dropping away. Alexandre's mother and father lived frugally without being poor; they expressed themselves simply without being stupid, existed without living. Their only son grew up with two hearts: one for his parents, and one for the outside world. The enclosed universe in which his mother and father existed, loving toward him despite everything, attentive in spite of their silence—their enclosed universe remained open for him; he could be the handsome, amiable boy in the village, and the quiet, dreamy child at home.

And so, Alexandre became the ideal young boy, and then the ideal adolescent. Mothers dreamed of finding him scrounging for snacks in their refrigerators; their sons invited him over after school, proud of his friendship. Even in primary school, girls eyed him with a desire they didn't understand. Alexandre was so nice, so polite. Not strong, just kind. He never got into fistfights, never played roughly, never found himself in a punch-up surrounded by a circle of eager spectators. No; Alexandre always remained outside the fray, dreaming of what his life would be when he grew up, of the meadow behind the house.

In class, he was a competent student without being the best, because he wasn't as intelligent as the mothers said; they were confusing politeness with refinement, good manners with good sense. He worked hard but never finished first in his class in either primary school or high school. One year, he managed ninth place, but never higher. It didn't matter; he was in the top third. His parents were astounded that he'd done so well;

having spent their own lives falling short of everyone else, it
had never occurred to them that their son might do better than
other children. They left him alone to do as he pleased. His
mother fixed breakfast for him every morning. When he got
up, a bowl and spoon were waiting for him on a neatly folded
cloth. They ate together in the evenings; if Alexandre
announced that he'd gotten a good grade his father said,
"Good," and if he confessed that he'd gotten a bad one his
mother said, "You'll do better next time." Alexandre loved his
parents because they never put any pressure on him to achieve
the success they had never had. They trusted him in an idle sort
of way, thinking, *He'll do fine*. The good qualities possessed by
their charming son had nothing to do with them; they discovered them at the same time as all the other parents, astonished
that he was their son, so firmly ensconced in their own defeat
that they couldn't imagine having passed anything on to him
except melancholy. And so, their love for him was a bit odd,
but it was sincere. He was their boy, and he would do fine, and
they would be proud of him if he wanted them to be proud of
him. It didn't matter to them that Alexandre wasn't at the top
of his class because he wasn't good enough to be there.
Something was missing in him: that extra bit of brilliance possessed by children who have already been through it all. He
lagged behind the best, and of the top three, only one was a
girl. Blanche Émard.

E veryone knew her story.

She had come back to class only a few days after her parents' car accident, looking daggers at anyone who stared at her, especially the boys. She waited for them to drop their gazes, and they did. "That girl will manage all right no matter what," her teacher told the mothers at the school drop-off when they expressed concern for Blanche and Gabriel. Émilienne patched up the children's wounds like a field surgeon lacking supplies; she made do with what she had: herself, her cows and chickens and pigs, her fields and her fireplace and her ponds. Her little band assembled each evening and scattered each morning, confident in its leader. Émilienne had the body of a starving ogress, tough and solid enough to withstand any test, equally capable of both tenderness and violence, caresses and slaps, and everyone around her relied on the support of that body to remain standing themselves.

Almost immediately, Blanche stood tall. She didn't need to try very hard to be among the best students in her class. And she was already working on the farm after school with Émilienne and Louis. Blanche had inherited her grandmother's common sense: learn fast or die. Learn fast or remain at the back of the herd—and remaining at the back at the herd, for an orphaned girl with no prospects but a farm and a lovesick farmhand, was unthinkable from the start. Blanche wasn't friendly, or gracious, or polite—but she was incredibly quick and clever, with a lively mind and a vibrant way of speaking. Like two workhorses, she and her grandmother towed Gabriel, an innocent boy broken by his parents' deaths, through the fields of his grief.

Even while still a little girl, she left the schoolyard the moment the final bell rang. Émilienne or Louis would be waiting for her at the gate and they would set off, silently, on the road to Paradise. Blanche always wore jeans, T-shirts, and sweaters, slightly too large but clean, her body pale and slender like the trunk of a young birch tree. The colors of her clothing—blue, black, or gray—accentuated the color of her eyes, enormous in her petite face, the little girl's face she would never lose, with a mouth bracketed by odd parentheses, as if old age had already staked a claim on her features, even in childhood. After her parents' deaths she remained in others' eyes a lonely child, stricken by loss at what should have been a time of normal and necessary innocence. This chaos had turned Blanche into a warrior at five years old.

When Alexandre and Blanche found themselves sitting next to each other in math class, they quickly formed a business relationship; she helped him with equations, while he sweet-talked his friends' parents into buying their eggs and poultry from Émilienne rather than the grocery store.

"I'll tell them the chickens from your farm might not be the biggest, but they're the best ones around."

"Have your parents ever bought chickens from us?"

"No. I'll have to stretch the truth a little."

It worked. Alexandre rose to fifth place in their math class. On Thursdays and Saturdays Émilienne sold more eggs and more lettuce and always received some orders for the following week. It all started that way, for the sake of a higher grade and a few eggs. Armed with his charming smile, Alexandre sang Émilienne's praises, often saying, "The tragedy that family's been through has only made her more hard-working." For her part, Blanche took the time to explain square roots to him, how to find the value of x, and which bracketed equation to solve first to simplify an algebraic expression. He wasn't as good as she was, of course, and she wasn't as good a salesman as he was. But she never gave him the answers during a test, even when he clasped his hands as if in prayer and gazed at her beseechingly. After class he followed her down the hall, murmuring:

"You could've given me the answers, really; what do you gain by making me lose points?"

She didn't turn around.

"You find answers, you don't ask for them. Either you're smart, or you're an idiot. If I give you the answer, you're an idiot."

He went quiet, crestfallen, trying to calculate his probable score on the test. Blanche would get a 16 or a 17, of course. She understood it all; she had an answer for everything. They walked together to their next class, where Blanche sat down in the second row and Alexandre in the first, listening to the teacher's comments on some book or another. Alexandre took notes, but he never read the books. Blanche listened closely and read every text more than once.

One evening, Louis was waiting for her at the gate, the car window rolled down. He watched as the two teenagers emerged from the schoolyard, Alexandre heading for the playing field. Louis knew the boy's parents; they were very quiet, and very sad. He had seen Alexandre at the market, too, extolling the virtues of what Louis generally sold with his hands in his pockets, forcing a smile, while this boy of sixteen spread his arms and invited his friends' mothers to buy Émilienne's poultry and lettuce and eggs. It bothered Louis, but he went along with it, amazed at the boy's talent, unable to figure out why this stranger who had never set foot in Paradise was bending over backward for the farm.

When he saw them that evening, for a few seconds at most, striding across the schoolyard side by side, sure-footed, almost triumphant, he knew that Blanche would never be his, that he didn't have the right even to think about it. He sat up straight behind the steering wheel, exhaling loudly and trying to blot the image of her pale thighs from his memory. And then an unbearable scene flashed through his mind, as assuredly as the boy had walked through the schoolyard: Blanche, being taken by Alexandre, outdoors, on the green grass of Paradise. He doubled over, feeling like he might go mad from pain, his gut twisting at the thought of the lovers, the curving shapes of their bodies.

"Are you sick?"

Blanche had stuck her head in the window. Louis looked up at her, anger flashing in his eyes.

"Queasy," he muttered.

She got into the car without another word. He stomped on the gas pedal.

"Be sure to thank your friend for that show he put on in the market," Louis said. The words came out in a hiss.

A half-smile crossed Blanche's face. A single parenthesis. Louis's favorite.

"It's working, isn't it?"

"We don't need it."

"Stop for a second."

Louis slammed on the brakes. The car came to a halt in the middle of the road. He sat with one hand on the steering wheel, the other clenched into a fist that Blanche stared at now, her eyes widening. It wasn't threatening her, this fist; it was a fist that wanted to hit someone else.

"He's not doing it for us," he said, between gritted teeth. "He's doing it for you."

Blanche blushed, but didn't look away. She wanted to laugh, but before the second parenthesis could make its appearance Louis started driving again, more slowly this time, saying only:

"He's a sixteen-year-old boy. Be careful. Émilienne will tell you the same thing."

Blanche settled herself in her seat. The seatbelt dug into her shoulder; her book bag held steady between her feet. She bit back her response. "You just wish you were in his place."

Alexandre had turned up in the early afternoon. Blanche was reading in her room. Louis sat at the dining room table, flipping through the newspaper. Émilienne was gutting a chicken in the kitchen sink, tugging at the entrails until they detached with a moist sucking sound.

Three knocks at the door.

"Go and open it, Louis."

Alexandre stood at the foot of the porch steps, his habitual, dimpled smile firmly plastered on, if a bit stiff.

"Sorry to bother you, but I was wondering if Bl—"

"Yes, Blanche is here; where else should she be?" Louis spat, looking away.

Alexandre nodded but didn't move. He was waiting for Louis to give his permission, while Louis himself was waiting for the boy to say something, but a sudden racket behind him made him sigh. In her room, Blanche had heard Alexandre's voice and, before Louis could say a word, he was elbowed aside by the girl, who stepped out onto the porch, pleased and surprised.

"What are you doing here?" she asked.

Louis had pushed the door behind them without shutting it completely. He stood and listened.

"What are you up to, Louis?" hissed Émilienne, a dishcloth in her hand.

He motioned for her to be quiet. She shrugged and moved closer to the door, leaning in to listen to the teenagers.

"D'you want to go out with me?"

Louis and Émilienne exchanged a look. Outside, Blanche,

frozen on the porch steps, stared at Alexandre as if she'd never seen him before. He'd spoken without taking his eyes off her, his cheeks dimpling, his lips curving in a charming smile. Alexandre didn't take a step toward her. He'd asked his question like a pupil asking his teacher for an explanation, and now he was waiting for that teacher, so lovely in her hesitation, to answer.

"Okay."

Louis stalked out of the vestibule and slammed the kitchen door. Émilienne, standing alone, staring at the doorknob, took a deep breath, her eyes closed. She shook her head once, banishing an unpleasant thought from her mind. Just as she was about to step out onto the porch and tell Alexandre to leave Paradise, she heard her granddaughter add:

"But you can't touch me until I say it's all right."

Émilienne opened the door wide. Alexandre turned and left the yard. Blanche watched him go. Émilienne was about to demand that she come back inside—it was almost dark—but then she spotted Blanche's left foot on the second step. When the girl turned to face her, Émilienne noticed that her lips were rosier than usual, a pretty pink flush glowing on her cheekbones.

They had kissed. Her granddaughter's green eyes were like two stars that had just exploded in the darkness. Émilienne couldn't bring herself to say *be careful*; not after this first kiss. She simply gave the girl a half-smile, the one that meant "we'll talk about this later," and instead of going back inside, where Louis was muttering over his newspaper, instead of plunging her large hands into the sink full of tepid water, she crossed the yard and headed for the pigpen.

A handsome boy, with a nice smile, and a pleasant voice, and ambition. Making her way toward the pen, Émilienne reflected that she couldn't blame Louis for loving Blanche, and she couldn't blame Blanche for loving Alexandre. It happens, sometimes, that things progress of their own volition, with no thought for who gets hurt, or will get hurt soon.

They touched, at last, a few months after Alexandre had come to Paradise. She refused to hold hands with him in the schoolyard, or the main street, or the little roads that branched off it. She always rebuffed him gently, saying she "didn't like how it felt to be touched like that." Alexandre never pushed the issue, his hand dangling awkwardly at his side, waiting for the mysterious moment when she would give the signal. He and Blanche worked together, ate lunch together, walked together; they were like a young old couple, so attractive—that was what the teachers and the other students thought; so attractive—but connected to each other only by words. Blanche would kiss him hello and goodbye; quick, dry pecks, on the cheek rather than the lips.

A Thursday in March. A bright late-winter sun shining. Bathed in white light, the façade of the high school was dazzling, the students shielding their eyes as they headed for the entrance. Blanche was out in front of the building, leaning against the wall, waiting for Alexandre to finish gym class.

He burst suddenly out of the school to her left, more quickly than usual. Breathless, he didn't even take the time to kiss her, pulling his latest report card from his backpack.

"You're my best teacher!" he declared, waving the paper beneath Blanche's nose.

Alexandre had risen two places in class. He was in the top three now.

"My best teacher, and definitely the prettiest," he added, winking.

Blanche seized the report card. Instead of turning away into the shadow of the wall so she could read the comments written beneath each column of results, she flung her thin arms around Alexandre's neck and kissed him, for real this time. Her mouth explored his for a long time, their lips moist, Alexandre's hands on her waist, his fingers pressing into her skin through her clothing, gently, as if he were afraid she might fall to pieces, or maybe this was a dream—but no, Blanche was really here, in his arms, in his mouth. The report card still clutched in her right hand, Alexandre felt her fingertips stroking the back of his neck, her tongue seeking his, gently coaxing. She seized Alexandre's hand and they set off down the main road together toward Paradise, where the young man would soon discover the upstairs bedroom with the big tree outside, safe from Louis's watchful gaze, safe from his own room in his parents' house, where he would have been ashamed to bring a girl or even a friend. His own room, which he wanted to leave behind more than anything in the world.

Fucking. They never used that word. They'd heard it, of course; heard it everywhere, all the time: on TV and the radio, in books and magazines, in conversations at the café and in the market and late at night, and from the back of the classroom and in the schoolyard and in homeroom. They heard it, but they never said it. When Alexandre was alone he spent hours thinking about Blanche, dressed or barely dressed, wearing only a single garment or even just her summer sandals; he imagined her taking pleasure from him, even though he never actually included himself in these scenes he drew in his mind until every muscle in his body was paralyzed with desire. He pictured Blanche, sometimes from behind, offering her backside to him; sometimes beneath him, her eyes closed, and him ordering her to open them so that he could see her pleasure in them; other times in strange positions, from the side, slightly twisted in on herself, so that the curve of her breasts seemed rounder, or the line from her neck to her shoulder straighter. Alexandre spent most of his time imagining Blanche. And when the images overwhelmed him and he came, in his sheets, or his hand, or the shower, or in a bathroom stall at school or even, once, on the side of the road where he had lain down among the tall stalks of a wheat field, even then, he was never thinking about "fucking" Blanche. Having her, taking her, filling her, holding her, maybe, yes—he had said these words in his head. But "fucking" her, no. The people who used that term were boys who had never fucked anything but their right hand, or men, dirty, drunk, lonely, and celibate, who couldn't even really remember what had, in that brief moment of their existence when women looked at them with desire, truly given rise to the giving or taking of pleasure. Alexandre was certain that using the word "fuck" was proof that you *didn't* fuck, and that it was bad for the mind, that it made you sick. Blanche would not make him sick; he would never think or speak of her like that, like a girl more "fuckable" than the rest.

It had taken some time for Blanche to let Alexandre get close to her, but once she accepted his hands on her, her apprehension evaporated the way fog dissipates and suddenly gives way to a clear, bright sky. Now, both of them were walking together through this life that had previously been pocked with dark holes and accidents and dim, confined houses, with the absence of money, with *absence*, period. If Louis was working outside when Alexandre came to visit Blanche, the boy was careful not to upset the chickens, not to disturb anything in the house, not to cause any change at all. He touched the farm lightly and he touched Blanche lightly, delicately, leaving no trace of his passage, knowing that his presence was new and probably unwelcome in the fragile state of equilibrium that Émilienne had painstakingly, laboriously established, aware that he posed a threat to that equilibrium. He was careful never to linger too long; he always brought sweets, fresh bread, cordial, butter. When she looked out the kitchen window and saw him crossing the yard, Émilienne never said anything. He walked carefully.

Alexandre avoided Louis, and Louis avoided Alexandre. At Paradise, in front of the high school, at the market, in the café, they spoke little, almost not at all, a curt, silent wave their only greeting to one another. Blanche went from one to the other like a rowboat between two riverbanks, seeing Louis the way she'd always seen him, as part of a family bound not by blood but by tragedy. She respected him but was careful to avoid saying or doing anything that might make him think she felt any more for him than that, or regarded him as more than the survivor of a drama that was still playing out in the little bungalow where he'd been born. Alexandre's arrival on the scene brought Louis even closer to Émilienne. The old lady knew what it cost him to be in the younger man's presence, and in the silent country air she urged him to stand firm the way she did, to keep going, not to let himself be mired down in the dark pits that were opening up in his life. Teaching him that learning to live meant stepping around these pits.

On the day the pig was butchered, as Blanche and Alexandre left the bedroom, Louis fell savagely on the animal, his hands drenched in blood, the way he would have done on his own father, or on the body of a girl he didn't love. The smell of the blood gave him strength and he inhaled it, drawing deeply, filling himself up with it so he wouldn't think about what they had done upstairs, in the very room where he had been cared for and loved for the first time. He stepped around the pit that his desire, his anger and rage, were causing to yawn beneath his feet. The men around him were praising him, calling him a "good lad" and suggesting that he come work for them occasionally. Louis replied that he didn't "work" here; that this was "his life, that's all," and in saying the words he realized that he wouldn't be able to raise or feed or kill animals that belonged to someone else. His hands sticky with blood, Louis felt like the guardian of Paradise. Necessary and needful.

Émilienne was aging. It wasn't that she ever complained, or walked more slowly, or balked at a task; no, it was just that Louis had noticed that she was out of breath when she came back up the hill from the pigpen, maybe went there a bit less often. Sometimes she'd sit down to rest or repeat the same thing several times. Louis heard her muttering secrets, talking to herself about her fears for the future, or the price of eggs or meat, or the weight of the cows, or the number of calves. He heard it, and it hurt him; he felt as if he wasn't a worthy enough

confidant for Émilienne's needs or her worries; that she preferred to talk to herself, her younger self, rather than sitting
down with Louis and asking him to take the reins from her in
her old age, leaning on his strong peasant's arms to maintain
the farm long enough for Blanche to finish high school and
learn from her grandmother how to keep Paradise going. Louis
knew that he and the eldest daughter of the Émard family
shared a deep physical attachment to the land of Paradise; consuming, voracious, untamable. Blanche would never leave.
Despite her excellent school marks and her teachers' urging to
pursue a successful future—she hated that word, "pursue";
like a hunter stalking an animal; they were pushing her to stalk
the outside world—Blanche would never abandon her grandmother or her brother in Paradise.

Gabriel was consumed with melancholy, in the way of children who have known shattering loss. Émilienne had been severe with him. Fair, but severe. She had left him outside to cry until he was drained of tears, of anger and violence, forgetting that tears and anger and violence are flowers that bloom all year round, even in dry eyes, even in bodies that are loved, even in hearts that have been patched back together.

Gabriel grew up distorted. He was polite, but his politeness was forced, the politeness of a person unable to think about anything but those who should be here but aren't; the politeness that means *please don't hurt me; I'm already damaged.* Émilienne, Blanche, and Louis worked endlessly, beasts alongside beasts, machines alongside machines, the industrious angels of this Paradise of mud and beaks and manure. Gabriel was thin, frighteningly thin. Émilienne fed him twice as much as his sister, but his body refused to fill out, his arms like two matchsticks with round pebbles glued to them for elbows, his impossibly long legs like stilts made of flesh and bone. From a distance, in a T-shirt, he looked like a tattered scarecrow mounted on a couple of poles, wandering through the tall grass, his arms held out in an embrace no blood parent could return. The future held no interest for him; it took the occasional slap from Émilienne or shove from Louis to make him move forward, like a sickly foal, along the path marked out by the Émard family's sorrows.

Friendless at school, talentless except for his knack for staying aloof, he was horribly calm, the calm of the grave, of a child who held his spine very straight, eyes cast down toward the ground or up to the sky, not looking at anything except measureless space, the ceiling of the heavens and the floor of the earth, trying to break through their surfaces to escape this world, his age, his family, his school; all the others, human and animal, the roads and prairies, the hills and the brooks. Everything was defined by lines and borders and signs: the body, the riverbank, footpaths and sidewalks and barbed-wire fences; everything had a direction and a form and a function. Gabriel stood in the middle of all this like something dropped there at random.

Small children thought Gabriel was bizarre, while the older ones called him a daydreamer. His body grew faster than he did. He was an odd sight, both as a little boy and a teenager, walking alone on the side of the rutted road to town, that potholed strip of black asphalt whose bends and curves, sometimes easy, sometimes dangerous, here a horseshoe, there a hairpin, led those who traveled it toward the confines of a horizon clotted with trees and low-roofed houses. Yes, he looked odd, as waiflike in his person as he was monumental in his grief, ambling along the verge. There was something of the animal about him, an animal sick with sadness and timidity. Émilienne and Blanche lived alongside him like two cats, going about their duties, occasionally throwing him a questioning glance, which he always answered with a shrug. His constant fatigue, his absolute lack of love and desire for this farm where he'd known the worst moments of his short life; all these things excluded him from this strange family, whom he loved, certainly, but whose arms were too full to gather him up in a hug.

Louis was different. In a way, he understood the boy's orphan grief. Every night, he sat down on the edge of Gabriel's bed with a simple "Good night; pleasant dreams," and every morning, he perched in exactly the same place at exactly seven o'clock. Gabriel would wake up, and Louis would already be dressed, smelling of hay. The boy would pry his eyes open and

the farmhand would say "Have a good day; stay out of trouble."
And then he'd leave the room, and the boy wouldn't see him
again until lunchtime. Those few words created an invisible
bridge between them where they sometimes found themselves
together, like two sad, sweet friends.

As a teenager, endowed with the intuition common to those
ravaged by depression, Gabriel realized before Blanche did—
and even before Louis—that the two of them could never be
brother and sister, or friends, or companions. None of those
things. He knew, because he understood his sister's rage and
Louis's suffering, that there was nothing aside from Émilienne
and Paradise keeping them in the same place. They were so different, so scarred by the respective horrors they had endured,
that they had mutually convinced themselves that no one
deserved their trust, their friendship, or their love. Gabriel
watched Louis fluttering in Blanche's orbit, watched his sister
flinching away from his touch, both with fangs bared, confusing
tenderness with a vicious bite.

Until Alexandre knocked on the door that day, Gabriel had
always thought of his sister like a malfunctioning robot. And
then he'd watched her get close to this handsome boy. Seeing
Blanche's heart touched despite her harshness had made her
brother less gloomy; discovering that she was capable of loving
something other than a farm made her seem prettier, made him
feel closer to her, and that idea soothed him, drove back the
nightmares. But even as Blanche became more human in his
eyes, Louis, defeated by Alexandre, battled with himself.
Gabriel heard him at night, in the grip of bad dreams; he
watched him during the day, plagued by dark thoughts. The
more Blanche loved Alexandre the more Louis hated himself,
while Gabriel observed them both from afar, alone in his room,
an actor refusing to play his part.

Even after having undressed and offered herself, after standing defiant beneath the gazes of others, especially Louis, Blanche acted as if nothing had changed within her. For weeks, she behaved rudely, accepting Alexandre's small gestures of affection in silence as they stood together at the edge of Sombre-Étang, the grebes dipping their little beaks in the water, feet paddling at right angles to the choppy surface. They filled the bedroom with their scents, wanting pleasure, wanting not to have pain anymore, the pain of the past, of the childhood that must be left behind, of Louis, of everything. Émilienne tolerated the teenage couple's presence under her roof so long as they pretended to evade her watchful eye; of course she knew they were upstairs, but Alexandre was so discreet, and Blanche so meticulously private, that she accepted their love-play while Louis sweated in the muck with the cows and the pigs, while Gabriel, in his room, ruminated over things she preferred not to think about. In the end, Blanche and Alexandre could spend hours, whole days entwined in Paradise; in the sighs and saliva, the soft laughter and the semen, it was life they brought to the place; finally, life. It was as simple as that.

Little by little, Blanche surrendered herself.

She took him into her confidence first. Just when he was least expecting it, in biology class. They were dissecting the corpse of a frog and Blanche, while extracting the animal's heart, murmured:

"Sometimes I wonder if the doctors did this to my parents."

Alexandre stopped short.

"When they were found," she continued. "I wonder if they were all cut open, like that"—she indicated the frog's thighs—"or if a doctor did it, or a cop."

Her voice was low, steady.

Alexandre didn't know what to say.

"I don't know," he stammered softly, leaning slightly toward her.

"I don't know either."

Then she straightened up, stretching, and seeming to yawn, though no sound escaped her lips. Just before the bell rang, she said:

"There are a lot of things I don't know about them."

They left the classroom together, Alexandre lagging a bit behind Blanche, watching her carefully. All around them, students were exchanging a barrage of insults, unbearably naïve and touching, the insults of boys and girls terrified by the idea of becoming men and women. Blanche and Alexandre never paid attention to any of it, regarding their schoolmates in the manner of annoyed hall monitors or indifferent teachers. They didn't belong to this world of textbooks and report cards and grades anymore, because their families—what was left of them—had forced them to create a future for themselves before the others. Fear had brought these two children into bed together; fear, and the rejection of the pain that blood inflicts, the absolute, insolent, terribly *living* refusal to go down without fighting, even against themselves.

Blanche slowed. She didn't take Alexandre's hand, and he didn't try to reach for hers. Their steps matched the rhythm of Blanche's voice, murmuring things about her parents, about life with them, and about Émilienne too. As she spoke, Alexandre stared at his feet, concentrating as hard as he could on each sentence, memorizing them, unable to say anything; he felt as if a single move, even a breath, would shatter the trust she was placing in him, the liberty she was taking, and the pain, the unutterable pain that was being released with her words, here on this ordinary walk from the high school to Paradise. Pain that overflowed in her pronunciation of her parents' first names, Étienne and Marianne. She never called them Mama and Papa.

"They died because of the road," she said, gesturing to the asphalt.

"What happened?" he asked, even though he knew the whole story already.

"The rain, and the bend in the road, over that way." Her index finger picked out a point on the horizon, beyond Paradise, sketching a sharp curve, trembling slightly.

"Who was driving?" Alexandre asked.

Now Blanche stalked ahead a few steps and then whirled to face him.

"Why does that matter?" she hissed.

Alexandre felt unbelievably stupid. He went to her and pressed his lips to her neck. She didn't move, her body neither yielding in forgiveness nor stiffening in rejection. His hands slipped down to her waist and he laid his head on her shoulder, and Blanche relaxed more quickly than he had expected. He felt her melt into him. After a few seconds she broke the odd embrace, and as they reached the turn onto the road, she breathed, softly:

"It had to be my mother."

The sun was setting, the green of Blanche's eyes deepening in the twilight. Before she set off down the path beyond Marianne's wooden sign, he said:

"All of this will be over soon, you know."

He beamed, the grin of a conquering hero, his face superbly handsome.

"Very soon. And we'll be able to leave."

She waved a hand dismissively.

"Out of the question," she said. "If I go, who will guard the gates of Paradise?"

Alexandre took a step backward.

"You've never dreamed of something else? Far away from here?"

He turned on his heel, tossing a slight nod over his shoulder and blowing a quick kiss in her direction.

The bales of hay stacked in the barn, bound with green cords, seemed light, as if they might collapse at any moment, but they never did. In truth, they were much heavier than they looked. When Blanche was little, she used to play with them, pushing as hard as she could on the bottommost one in the pile, arms straining with the effort. She would throw all of her weight against the unmoving bale, her left leg taut, heel digging into the ground, right leg flexed at the knee, shoulders hunched, trying with all her might to move the bale. She sweated, grunted, the wall of hay scratching her hands, her fingers sinking into it, tiny insects skittering up her arms. She would end up panting, her hair a tangled bird's nest atop her small head, the stack of hay bales towering over her. She knew perfectly well that she couldn't move a wall that size with her strength alone, but she wore herself out trying, and that soothed her.

A few days after the frog-dissecting session, Blanche went into the barn. She glanced around the yard, fearful of being seen, and took a firm grip on the second hay bale from the bottom, climbing easily up the stack of rolled bales, dry, prickly strands clinging to her clothing. Reaching the top of the pile, she settled herself comfortably and took a deep breath.

It was almost the end of the year. Teachers were asking the best students to see them after class so they could "talk about the future," and yesterday had been Alexandre's turn. Blanche had seen him waiting in the hall, excited as a worm wiggling on a fishhook, shifting from one foot to the other in front of the door. She'd just been coming up behind him when the lead hall monitor had come out of a classroom at the other end of the corridor; Alexandre had waved to her so enthusiastically, so easily, so warmly that Blanche had come to a dead stop. The young woman had smiled with pleasure and held out a hand, first and middle fingers crossed—*Good luck, Alexandre*, it meant—and a wave of jealousy had swept over Blanche, standing frozen behind her boyfriend. Suddenly she felt very young, and very stupid. Alexandre wasn't even eighteen yet, but women already saw him as a grown man. This hall monitor believed in him; she was supporting his hopes and nurturing his ambitions. Blanche felt humiliated, tossed aside in a world she'd always dismissed, one which, as adulthood knocked at the door of adolescence, had suddenly become so attractive to Alexandre. Now the classroom door opened, and the boy stepped inside proudly, confidently. Blanche had heard him speaking to the teacher for a few seconds. She had wanted to press her ear to the keyhole, but some students had come down the stairs just then, their voices had drawn her backward, away from this Alexandre whom women eyed with such desire.

A solitary queen atop her tower of hay, Blanche relived the scene now, burning at the memory of the hall monitor's encouraging gaze, of Alexandre fidgeting with anticipation, shifting his weight from foot to foot. Nausea gripped her and she flung herself onto her back on the hard-packed hay. She was like a heavy winter coat, cumbersome, pleasant to wear, but heavy. She'd always thought she was Alexandre's dream. The rest seemed marginal, unimportant. Until yesterday, she'd never imagined a future for them other than Paradise, the bedroom, the cows, the coffee on the table. Love.

She flattened her palms against the surface of the hay, pressing hard to feel the sprigs of it biting into her skin. A shiver ran through her wrist and up her forearm. A spider, round and black, crept in fits and starts up her elbow, lifting its tiny claws high with each step. Blanche found it almost beautiful in the half-light. A strange feeling rose slowly from somewhere deep within her. She sat up carefully, so as not to disturb the spider in its progress along her elbow; then, suddenly, she began to tremble. Feverishly, she imagined crushing it with a single press of her thumb, just for the pleasure of doing it. As if the creature had sensed the threat, it jumped from her arm and skittered to the edge of the haystack, and Blanche sighed with relief. Her heart thumped to the rhythm of the spider's steps; a series of images flitted through her head, she could have killed it, felt its flesh and blood mingling beneath her fingertips. For an instant, the round, black body was replaced by the hall monitor's face. A second later, Émilienne was calling her from the porch.

W hat were you thinking?"
In the passenger seat, Gabriel stared down at his lap. Louis, both hands on the steering wheel, bit his lower lip hard enough to draw blood. Gabriel, unmoving, knew he was holding back a barrage of curses.

"Honestly, Gabriel, I would have understood this coming from your sister, but you?!"

The school had called Paradise an hour ago. Gabriel had attacked a classmate. No one had ever seen the timid child in such a rage. Christophe, a stocky older boy Gabriel knew by sight because they were both at the market every week, had broken up the fight.

He'd been waiting at the school gate. When Louis got out of the car, Christophe shook his hand warmly and asked him what he'd "been doing with himself."

"Go easy on him," he said, watching Gabriel climb into the passenger seat. "It was just a little scrap."

"Has he been punished?"

"A warning."

The boy sat still, head down.

"I'll deal with it. Thanks, anyway."

"No problem. Gabriel's not a bad kid."

The bell rang. Blanche and Alexandre would be out in a few minutes.

Louis heaved a sigh and got into the car, slamming the door. Hordes of teenagers were filing past outside, some of them walking ahead, proud and sure of themselves. Alexandre was like that already, he thought. Fearless.

"Why aren't you starting the car?"

Gabriel had spoken without looking up. The words came out softly, slowly.

"I'm taking Blanche back too."

Louis asked Gabriel twice to explain the fight, and both times the boy simply shook his head, as if trying to shoo away the questions, refusing to say anything at all. When Blanche came through the gate, Louis sighed again. The boyfriend was trotting at her heels, and when he'd slipped into the back seat of the car on the passenger side he leaned forward and said, cheerfully:

"He had it coming, Gabriel! You were right."

The boy was visibly gloating. There was a triumphant smile on his handsome face. Louis sought Blanche's gaze in the rearview mirror. She had her eyes closed, lulled by the car's movement, allowing herself to be driven. Alexandre kept squeezing Gabriel's shoulders, repeating, "Good job, good job," despite Louis's clear exasperation. When they pulled up in front of the road leading to Paradise, the farmhand asked, without waiting for Émilienne's permission or Blanche's:

"You want to stay for dinner tonight?"

Alexandre stopped midsentence.

"Are you sure, Louis?" Blanche asked, sleepy-voiced.

"Absolutely sure. You've been together for a while now, and around here"—Louis flicked a glance at Alexandre—"we show respect to people who've become part of the family."

Alexandre laughed.

"I'd love to!"

Louis drove down the road, dirt clods and pebbles turning the car into a rattletrap. The farmhand's eyes glittered. He led the herd; Alexandre, his head sheep, followed docilely. After he'd parked, he instructed Gabriel to go and warn his grandmother. Then he vanished behind the barn.

*

Alexandre ran his hands along his girlfriend's waist, murmuring:

"We've got time, don't we?"

"Yes, but I don't want to," she said, disentangling herself from his embrace.

Alexandre stood alone on the porch. Blanche's refusal had done nothing to dampen his enthusiasm. Enchanted, he turned and gazed out at Paradise. The fields were bursting with spring colors, the forest humming with birds. Alexandre swept his hand across the landscape. Just then, Blanche's brother tripped slightly on a step. Alexandre could hear the boy breathing behind him; he knew Gabriel wanted to say something—to thank him, maybe, for his support in the car.

"Does the whole school know already?" the boy asked, finally.

The chickens were gathering near the gate.

"You never do anything, so word gets around pretty fast when you do."

Gabriel stared at Alexandre's body, his adult male body, sure that his own body would never look like that.

"He was saying stuff about my parents."

Alexandre turned suddenly to face him.

"It was just to get you riled up. Don't be stupid."

Gabriel sniffed. Fat tears, like the ones his grandmother had left him to cry himself all out of that night, here on this very porch, rose in his throat. Alexandre didn't want to touch him or even look directly at him. Gabriel was too fragile for that kind of attention. Before going into the house to find Blanche, he murmured:

"Don't think about it anymore."

É milienne was the last to sit down.

The week's leftovers, in a large casserole dish: potatoes, carrots, tomatoes, zucchini, chicken stock. The carcass tossed outside, in front of the barn, for the dog. At one end of the table, a basket of thick-sliced bread, dark brown, almost black.

Gabriel's gaze shifted discreetly from Émilienne to Alexandre. When he'd informed his grandmother that they had a guest for dinner a couple of hours ago, she hadn't even asked his name.

Louis occupied the "father's" place at the table, Gabriel sitting obediently next to him. Blanche and Alexandre sat across the table, their backs held very straight, the girl hiding her nervousness with difficulty, her legs jiggling under the bench. She hadn't said anything since the car ride home. Something was building within her, like a wave rising; Louis could sense it roiling inside her. Alexandre seemed indifferent; he was glowing, even more than usual, delighted to be there, though slightly discomfited by Émilienne's silence from the head of the table, where she presided over this odd gathering, passing plates and dishes, observing. Émilienne didn't ask him any questions; she simply let him speak, smiling occasionally when he mentioned his teachers. Here the young man was in the spot Blanche had set aside for him, the one Louis would never occupy. When the farmhand offered him a glass of wine, Alexandre refused.

"You act like the lord of the manor," said Louis, teasingly, but with an edge in his voice, "and yet you can't handle alcohol?"

The other young man smiled.

"I don't need that to give me courage," he said lightly, reaching for the pitcher of water.

Louis grunted and drained his glass but, to Blanche's surprise, didn't refill it.

"Did something happen today?" asked Émilienne.

Gabriel shrank back in his chair. Louis and Blanche hesitated. The old lady looked at them both and then her eyes shifted to Gabriel, who was pushing his potatoes around his plate, trying to remove himself from the conversation.

"Well?" she pressed, suspicion mounting in her voice.

Before Louis could say a word, Alexandre leaned forward in his chair and said, unbelievably:

"Yes, something happened: Blanche and I got our results!"

Gabriel let out a long breath. Louis elbowed him, just hard enough to make him sit up straight and take a bite of his vegetables.

Émilienne gave a soft whistle, part scoffing, part satisfied. Neither she nor Louis ever asked Blanche about her grades or her teachers' approval; they already knew what her answers would be. Hard-working student. Excellent results.

"Not now, Alexandre."

Blanche was shaking her head like a horse irritated by its halter. Émilienne opened her mouth to intervene, but Louis held up a hand and said, his voice a bit sharper now:

"Blanche is used to getting good marks—but it must be quite a shock for you, eh, my friend?"

Alexandre nodded.

"Oh, yes," he said, very seriously. "It's thanks to Blanche that I'm third in our class."

He rested a hand on his girlfriend's back as he said the words. She flinched. Trapped, Blanche stood and picked up her plate, keeping her hands busy, while Louis looked Alexandre right in the eye.

"So, what are you going to do with them? Your good little schoolboy's grades?"

Émilienne let out a soft snort, annoyed by the conversation. Gabriel loaded his fork with carrots.

Alexandre's eyes gleamed.

"I'm starting a business course in September."

There was a sound of crockery breaking. They all turned, silently, gripped by a sense of foreboding. Blanche stood in the passage leading from the dining room to the kitchen, her body stiff, her fingers still curled as if holding an invisible plate, staring at Alexandre, her bare feet littered with wet shards of ceramic.

"Does that mean you're going away?"

Émilienne made a move as if to rise. Blanche ignored her.

"You could stay, but you're going to leave?"

Alexandre got up and walked toward her, his mouth twisted in an apologetic smile.

"You'll hurt yourself."

He knelt and gathered up the pieces of the plate, setting them one by one on the table. Louis refilled his glass. Émilienne shot him a dark glance. He shrugged.

"You could stay," Blanche said again in a strangled voice.

She hadn't moved.

"We'll talk about it later."

"You brought it up!" she snarled, pushing him away.

Louis stifled a nervous laugh. Émilienne shot up from her chair, seized Blanche by the arm, and pushed her back against the wall. Her granddaughter was quivering with fury.

"Blanche, it's not a big deal. Calm down."

"It *is* a big deal."

Alexandre stared at Blanche as if he were seeing her for the first time. He took a step toward her, but Émilienne held up a restraining hand.

"Blanche, it's only three years," he murmured, chagrined.

"I'll be back on the weekends, and you can come see me during the week—"

She exploded, shrieking hideously. Suddenly, the air in the house seemed saturated with her anger; the others were petrified, gawking at her transformation, rage magnifying the power of her young body, so fragile, so incapable of violence. Her grandmother held on to her with all her strength, to keep her from launching herself at Alexandre. Gabriel huddled in his chair, terrified, and Louis stood and glared threateningly at the young man, emboldened by the full force of his love for Blanche.

"I *can't* leave, and you won't come back! You hate this place! You hate your parents! You hate everything here!"

Gabriel wanted to go to his sister, to tell her that he understood, that he screamed and wept sometimes, too. At that precise moment, he was the only one who could have calmed her, but he didn't move. Holding back despite himself, resigned, he waited for his sister's choking cries to drown out her words. The sound grew louder and louder, like a flock of frenzied birds. Alexandre, thunderstruck and shaking, stared at this seventeen-year-old witch.

Blanche sobbed, hiccupping, for a long moment, caught between Émilienne's heavy body and the stone wall, its coolness vying with the terrible heat burning in her cheeks, her skull, her hands. Louis took a step toward Alexandre.

"Get out," he hissed quietly.

HEALING

Blanche became a shadow. A dutiful, plodding, closed-off shadow, a shadow of rage and abandonment. She moved through her life like a ghost in a fortress, skulking in the shadows, sinking into darkness, becoming invisible to Louis, Émilienne, and Gabriel, who had watched her fall and fade. They didn't avoid the subject; it was just that they had experienced the disintegration along with her, Émilienne holding her pressed to the wall, Louis throwing Alexandre out of Paradise, Gabriel haunted by the same past, their shared past, the deep wound of unbearable separation.

Alexandre would not come back. Blanche knew it. He might come back the first weekend, maybe, but after that? The high life. "Real life," he called it. Maybe he thought he could be both at once, a city boy and a country boy, an ambitious man and an amorous one, a prodigal son and a loving one, but Blanche knew, from the way he talked about his parents, his "poor" parents and their "small" house, that there was nothing left for him here, really. There was only her, and she couldn't leave Paradise; Alexandre had known that from the beginning—she would never leave Émilienne, Gabriel, the pigs in the pen and the chickens in the yard. She couldn't follow him, because that would mean leaving Émilienne to die, Louis to grow old, Gabriel to suffer. What would become of Paradise, if Blanche left? Even for only a year, or two, or three? Louis, alone, would take care of the animals and the buildings and the fields. Émilienne, hunched over the big dining-room table, would calculate what the farm brought in each week, and what it cost, thinking they would have to hire someone, but knowing they couldn't. Gabriel could have stepped into Blanche's role, but he wasn't capable of it, of course he wasn't; you can't run an estate with your eyes full of tears.

If he hadn't gone away to "learn how to sell" in the city, Alexandre could have worked here, alongside Blanche. But he couldn't, and it wasn't because his body was unfit for hard work—on the contrary—but Alexandre wasn't a boy of the farm, of eggs and cattle, Alexandre wasn't a boy of marshes and manure and frogs; Alexandre was a restless man whose all-consuming dreams went far beyond the borders of Paradise, and his love for Blanche, his teenage love, intense and dazzling, wasn't enough to pin him down here, near his poor parents and their narrow little house, near Émilienne's old age and Louis's black looks, near the daily melancholy of Gabriel, whom he avoided at all costs, afraid of being infected by his sadness. Blanche was the only glimmer of light in that green and brown, gray and pallid, drought-stricken or storm-soaked expanse. And she had driven him away.

The young woman became a shadow, and like all shadows in ancient houses and vast landscapes, she didn't sleep. She filled a space and abandoned it all in a split second, elusive, endlessly compelled by her own heartache. She sustained herself with what was left over, moving in the wake of others, drinking after others had satisfied their thirst, stretching herself endlessly between the places of the past and those of the future. Everything began and ended in Paradise, named by an absent mother and made a mockery of by a lover, young and audacious, so beautiful when he laughed, so shameful in his imploring demands. Like a shadow, Blanche enveloped the farm in her silence, noiselessly crossing the yard, feeding the pigs and the chickens and the cows without a word. The animals watched her, ears lowered, nostrils quivering, shying away slightly from her mechanical movements. The hay raked, the grain scattered, the waste discarded. The bucket handle that made a rusty bracelet on the wrist; the fingers closed around the neck to snap it with one quick, efficient twist; the shovel slid carefully beneath the cow manure so as not to lose any. Louis tried to keep her from exhausting herself with difficult tasks at first, but she brushed off his concern. As time passed, as the end of the school year arrived, as the students accepted to colleges and universities gathered in the schoolyard and chattered in great excited bursts about places to stay in the city and ways of traveling there and back and keeping in touch, as those who, like Alexandre, had chosen to leave this place paraded through the schoolyard like soldiers off to fight and conquer, Louis stopped shielding her from the pain of hard work, from predawn awakenings and brief nights. He took a step back, watching the shadow without trying to touch it, sometimes following it at a distance, afraid it would tear and come apart.

After that catastrophic family dinner, Alexandre tried several times to explain himself to Blanche. He followed her through the halls at school, asking if they could "talk," and even as he was laying himself bare, pursuing her in her endless flight from him, listing the ways they could stay "in touch"— he'd already stopped using the word "together"; it was always "in touch"—he was confronted with a face he didn't recognize, closed, threatening. Alexandre tried to persuade Blanche. Always that broad smile, those beautiful eyes, that boyish expression that made people forgive him anything— and all were met with the same response from her: silence. Alexandre wondered if she was listening to him, if something in her was keeping her from seeing him, hearing him, talking to him. He even came back to the farm, but Louis chased him off, also in silence. Alexandre's smile, his beauty, his love, his tenderness—none of them did him any good at all. For

Blanche he was already gone, his abandonment of her already in the past.

How do you heal from a living love? Every day after Alexandre's departure, Émilienne mended the rifts, the cracks that this boy had opened in Blanche. She changed her grand-daughter's bedsheets to get rid of his scent. She awoke before Blanche—sometimes she didn't even go to bed at all—to make sure the girl would have a sumptuous breakfast waiting for her when she got up, despite the fact that it usually went untouched. The fruit was sliced into perfect half-moons, the coffee hot but not scalding, the slices of bread and butter with honey lined up perfectly on her plate. Émilienne washed Blanche's clothing every day, asking Louis to buy secondhand books at the market, hoping they might take her granddaughter's mind off things. In the morning, Blanche's boots and sandals and little canvas sneakers were perfectly clean on the front porch; her bed linen perfumed with lavender in the evening. On Friday, which had been her bath day since infancy, Émilienne crushed mint leaves and set them burning in a little candle diffuser on the side of the tub, adding thyme honey to the steaming water, washing Blanche's hair with egg yolk and sugar. *Mending* Blanche. Repairing her. The aged fingers massaged her skin, eased the tangles out of her hair, smoothed her sheets; the wrinkled lips warmed her cheeks with kisses, smiled whenever she passed, moistened the thread to patch her trousers. For his part, Gabriel took advantage of the silence that hung over the place to sink further into his dreams, never understanding why he had never been given the same care, devoid of jealousy, agreeing, like a dutiful little ox, that his sister was the key cog in their machine, and that none of the other three members of the household would survive her collapse if she failed to summon the strength to hoist herself out of the abyss into which Alexandre's departure had plunged her. She worked, admittedly. As hard as Louis; maybe harder. But she couldn't bring herself to show her face in the village, or deal with customers, or speak to former classmates, or ask for change at the baker's. She toiled within a very limited sphere, never venturing beyond the borders of her own grief.

Alexandre left the village in June. He had found a summer internship with a real estate agency in the city, which would allow him to pick up some pointers before entering business school. It would look good on his record, a young man of eighteen spending his summer in an office, learning.

Turning his back on the suffocating little house of his child-hood, Alexandre carried with him a single, unshakeable certainty that, despite the sense of failure, despite the memory of that last evening at Paradise, filled him with strength, assurance, self-confidence: he had loved Blanche, but he didn't love the place to which she was so devoted. Not as much as she did, anyway. He couldn't understand that there was no Paradise for the girl other than the one that harbored her rage and her suffering. With the incradicable talent for living that protected him and saved him from everything, even the disaster of his first love, he left her there, driven away by himself, by his own ambitious soul.

Y ou'll never guess."
Blanche was plucking a chicken, its feet dangling limply over an unfolded newspaper, her hands working with the regularity of a sewing machine, tugging and tossing and tugging again at the skin of the headless bird. The years had elongated her fingers, daily hard work gnarling them until they were like talons, phenomenally strong. The backs of her hands, tanner than any other part of her body, were already covered with little brown marks. Scars, sunburn, nicks, and scratches, minor cuts, Blanche's hands had been sculpted by animal feet, hooves, and claws; they no longer bore any resemblance to the teenage fists that had grasped Alexandre's hair as he trailed his tongue along her thighs for the first time. The part of Émilienne concealed by childhood had risen to the surface, showing on the backs of those hands. Soon more of her would emerge, her expressions, her posture echoing more clearly in the heaviness of the bust, in the fold of skin sketching a line between the eye and the ear, in the slightly drooping mouth and thin lips. For now, though, only Blanche's hands had been touched by the beginnings of old age, or "oldness," as Émilienne called it: peasant's hands, as powerful as a man's, a soldier's, a farmer's. Immense hands, incisive, capable of gentleness every now and then, when the heart called for a caress, along a horse's back, or a child's hair.

Blanche had turned thirty in April. To mark the occasion, Émilienne had left an envelope on her pillow, a bit of money "to buy whatever she wanted"; the note accompanying the sheaf of bills—as smooth and dry as if they'd been ironed—instructing her "not to buy anything for the farm." It was for her. For a new dress, a new pair of shoes to match, or a nice bottle of wine, some books, a round-trip train ticket to the city. At thirty, it would never have occurred to Blanche to spend a single sou for her own pleasure. She had blushed on reading the note, of course, like a teenager given permission to go out that evening, and then Louis had called from the courtyard for her to come down, that the eggs weren't going to sell themselves. Downstairs, Émilienne, weary but tenacious, bent but upright, had given her a wink before watching her head outside. A prisoner of her eighty-four years, Émilienne was storing herself up for the winter like an animal, leaving the two sturdy adults to pilot the stationary vessel that was Paradise. A few months earlier, she had still been asking Blanche or Louis to describe their day in detail—were the heifers and the bulls and the calves healthy? Were the sows eating well? The hens laying enough eggs? Had they fed the dog and put it on a new rope?—and each evening they'd complied patiently, rewinding the past twenty-four hours, hoping they hadn't forgotten to close a door or give the correct change or pour the right grain into the right trough. But they never forgot anything. And when Émilienne had slipped the ten twenty-franc bills into that envelope for Blanche, something collapsed inside her. Thirty years. How old had Marianne and Étienne been when they were killed in that road accident? How old?

Émilienne had crept softly up the stairs to place her gift on her granddaughter's pillow. Blanche had overcome the deaths of her parents; she had resisted Louis's desire, accepted her brother's helplessness. And above all, Blanche had stricken down her first love.

"You'll never guess!"

Louis sat down next to the young woman and began clearing the feathers from the table.

"Why am I even putting newspaper down if you're going to pick them up one at a time?"

Louis sighed and scooted closer to her, mischievously. Curiously, the years sat easily on him; the shadows of the past had lifted, leaving only the occasional trace, a slight quiver of the lip, perhaps, but he didn't seem to age. Now past forty, his hair, bleached pale by years of work in the fields, brightened his face. Blanche found him almost handsome when the sun shone on his hollow cheeks and kindled a gleam in his eye of something almost like joy.

"Cat got your tongue?"

Blanche picked up a handful of feathers and blew them in his face. Louis snorted and let out a sneeze, making the feathers flutter around the body of the hen, now pink and cold.

"What, did we get rich overnight?" she quipped, a teasing little nothing.

"Better! Gabriel has a girlfriend! Finally!"

Blanche's hand froze above the newspaper. Her eyes widened.

"A real one?"

Louis laughed.

"Of course, a real one! It's the girl from Le Marché. You know; the short one, with the boobs."

He thrust out his chest, cupping both hands in front of it.

"I know perfectly well who she is, thank you. No need for a visual aid."

Louis gazed into the fireplace, his stare unfocused. He was obviously imagining his head buried between those two magnificent breasts, and Blanche's mouth twitched with irritation.

"Louis, are you listening to me? What's she like, this girl? Other than her chest, which you seem to be quite familiar with."

He reddened and looked away, scratching at the table with the tip of a feather larger than the others.

"She's cute. Her father works at the train station, not far away."

He almost said, "with Alexandre's father." Blanche folded the four corners of the newspaper together.

"Will she chew him up and spit him out, do you think?" she asked, picking up the chicken and thrusting a hand inside its carcass, drawing a groan of disgust from Louis, his thoughts jerked unpleasantly away from the luscious bosom of the girl from Le Marché.

"She won't chew him up; she'll swallow him whole!"

Blanche smiled.

"He had his arms around her waist this morning," he continued.

She told him to be quiet. The older he got, the more he talked. A real chatterbox.

So, Gabriel had found someone to share his depression. She emptied the entrails into a dish for the dog.

"Promise not to make fun of him when he tells us."

Louis pretended to cross his heart. The news had visibly filled him with an almost ridiculous energy. Gabriel had found someone. Who would have thought it? Then again, he was an extremely handsome young man. Despite the passing years, he looked as much like a teenager as ever. At twenty-seven, he could pass for seventeen. He didn't go out much, so his skin had a dreamy pallor, and that paleness, along with his deep, serious eyes, turned every word he said into a sermon. He was like an angel crossing the yard of Paradise each day, with his uncombed hair, his rumpled trousers, his shirts with their buttonless cuffs flapping around his thin wrists.

Gabriel didn't live at Paradise anymore. Not in Émilienne's house, at least.

Upon finishing high school, he had shut himself in his room upstairs for months. Blanche's little brother had wanted to be alone. He hadn't wanted to see a soul. Émilienne had left him to his sorrows, which she couldn't understand, or perhaps understood all too well. She knew he would emerge when the time was right, and the summer he turned nineteen, he had announced that he was going to find work in the village. He would rent the tiny house across the road—more a box than a house—so as not to be too far away, he said. He'd told them this one evening after a dinner he hadn't touched, and when he'd stood up and spoken, a defiant look on his face, Louis had whistled admiringly.

"You felt you needed to stand up to tell us you're moving across the street?" Émilienne had asked, dryly.

Blanche hadn't said anything. She'd given him a look full of affection—not love, but affection—which he had returned distractedly, already elsewhere in his head.

And he had left. He had actually done it. He'd been a gofer at the bistro and then taken the night shift in the back room at the post office. He'd cleaned streets and dishes and toilets, and then he'd taken a job detasseling corn, and Émilienne had been sure he wouldn't be able to keep up the pace, skinny and weak as he was. But, as soon as he'd found himself outside Paradise, Gabriel had begun to draw on reserves of strength his grandmother and sister didn't know he had. When the summer season ended, after having paid two months' rent in advance, he had moved with nothing, absolutely nothing, into the little wood-and-cement cube on the other side of the bend in the road where his parents had been found dead.

From that day on, it had been his habit to drop by Paradise to "say hello," asking how things were going, sometimes staying for a coffee. But he never said much about himself or gave straight answers to Émilienne's questions. He came, that's all; simply came and showed himself to be healthy, to be managing, managing better than he had ever done at home. He wasn't happy, or even unburdened, exactly, but there was a sort of lightness in his way of arriving each evening at seven. Maybe living away from Paradise had brought him a kind of welcome anonymity, opened up a space within him, a place for thoughts and memories belonging only to him. Away from the watchful eyes of Blanche and Émilienne, away from the room he had shared with Louis, Gabriel—finally—grew up.

No one had commented when he'd moved across the road. Émilienne had asked Louis not to say anything, and when Louis had asked why she'd replied, "You know," her tone irritated, almost sad. Louis had stopped by Gabriel's place often at first, asking if he needed anything, or if he'd like to take a stroll together, or go for a beer. He always found Gabriel lounging on his bed or ensconced in his armchair, very calm, and the young man always answered, "No, but I appreciate it." Not "No, thanks," but "No, but I appreciate it," in a new voice, the voice of someone who had found a place of his own in the world. A small, shabby place, perhaps, but a place of his own. He felt almost as if he'd been born a second time, and after a few weeks, Louis had stopped visiting him. He still kept an eye out for Gabriel in the village and watched him when he was at Paradise in the evenings, like a bird hovering over a dark forest. Eventually, though, Louis had to reconcile himself to the idea that the boy was all right. Not perfectly fine, but all right, simply all right.

And now he was embracing a girl, and now there was a girl walking with him. Gabriel was living in his cube beyond The Pin, with his dreams and his silences, and now here was a girl, ready to share those dreams and those silences.

Gabriel had always drawn. Since earliest childhood, since Louloute's death, his hand had endlessly sketched sweeping lines on scraps of paper and whole pages and walls. Émilienne said he took after his father, that he was the same type, with the same messy hair, the same absentmindedness, and that he'd been knocked down in the dirt at an early age, too, just like him. And now a girl, a pretty girl, had come to lift him up.

As was his habit, Gabriel now stepped quietly and unobtrusively into the dining room. Blanche, still in shock, stared at him with wide, shining eyes.

"You certainly look pleased," her brother said, taking off his shoes even though he'd already tracked dirt into the vestibule.

"She only just heard the news," Louis said, teasingly.

Blanche looked daggers at him. He sat down next to her at the table, his expression uncomprehending.

"Is that what's making you so happy?"

Blanche laughed, both hands in the carcass.

Gabriel shot a glance at Louis, who caught it like a knife thrown across the room. Blanche's brother stared questioningly at the farmhand now, brows knitted.

Louis blew out a breath. "Fine, okay; I told her. But I saw you both outside the school this morning; it's not like you're hiding away."

Gabriel sighed. Blanche thought he would start telling them about the girl, but he seemed to close himself off. She pulled her right hand out of the bird's carcass, her palm dripping with blood and juices. Gabriel avoided her eyes. If he could have left the room; if only he could have left the room.

"What's wrong?" she asked. "You look so serious all of a sudden."

Louis opened his mouth to make one of his jokes, but Blanche silenced him with a look.

"I thought you meant something else," Gabriel said, uncomfortably.

Louis let out a *pfff*. He generally knew everything that was going on.

"What are you talking about?"

Gabriel turned and stared into the cold fireplace, his gaze lost among the ashes.

"Alexandre is back."

P eople loved his wide smile, the dimples that framed his mouth, giving his face a boyish look that made them trust him immediately: *This young man could never be anything but good and kind.*

Alexandre had lost none of his charm; if anything, he had added to it, building battlements of friendliness, of promises that fell softly on the ear. He spent his life scrutinizing the gazes of others, their movements, the meandering intricacies of their souls, in order to slip inside them, smoothly and softly, with that ease that was as extraordinary as it was wounding and cruel. This was the key to his ability to make deals rapidly, to obtain signatures within just a day or a week, checks he promised to deposit "whenever is best for you, of course." Everyone praised his manners; the man who had agreed to take him on as a summer intern fresh out of high school had been sufficiently impressed by his protégé's sharpness to keep him on for two years in a work-study program. Then he'd hired the young man on the spot. For twelve years, Blanche's great love worked for the same company, owned by the same family for three generations.

He sold office space, land, apartments, houses, garages, and businesses. At first, he worked solely by telephone; his voice soothed his customers' anxieties with the same reassuring frankness he'd conveyed selling eggs in the market as a teenager. Of *course* the apartment keys could be available a week earlier; of *course* the house was sound, the roof redone; of *course* the plot of land just outside the city was zoned for construction. Every sentence, every answer started with *of course*. And it worked. It didn't matter that the roof was full of holes the size of your fist, or that the land was on a flood plain, or that the apartment stank of dampness; those two magic words made it all go away. *Of course, ma'am. Of course, sir.* Even better, no one ever blamed him for anything. He was so young, so charming, his eyes so full of disingenuous honesty; who on earth could be angry with him over a few little fibs? Of course, Alexandre was the man for every occasion.

Eight years after he began working for the company, they sent him to New Zealand for a month to find the mysterious heir of a family whose only son had gone to sea years earlier, and whose inheritance constituted a financial gold mine for the firm. Once there, Alexandre located the man in question, struck up a friendship with him, and spent some considerable time roaming with him around the southern part of the country, its coast lined with abandoned properties left to rot. Alexandre made a deal with his host: he would buy a parcel of beachfront land, which the heir would live on and care for, and Alexandre would look after the family residence in France so that it could be sold at a good price. He returned from New Zealand the owner of a dozen hectares that would, in twenty years' time, be worth ten times what he'd paid for them, and the heir, on his gigantic island, knew that a young man was working busily to ensure that he'd have a nest egg for his old age. He trusted Alexandre. Just like everyone did.

After his return to France, Alexandre kept up a regular correspondence with the heir. While the other man maintained the property in New Zealand, Alexandre carried out improvements on the outside of the family residence, had the lawns mowed and the hedges trimmed, the floors redone, and the walls painted. Nothing too major. Nothing beyond the capacities of the men he habitually called on whenever a property required quick renovation for resale. He even lent a hand at the worksite sometimes, to show that he paid attention to everything, down to the smallest detail. The faulty plumbing was left untouched, as was the antique wiring. From the outside, to an untrained eye, this was an impeccably maintained house. It was sold three years after Alexandre's return, to a couple from out of town who fell in love with the immaculately landscaped garden. The gate was new; the windows had been replaced; there wasn't even a single dead leaf on the path to the front door. A wonder. For sale. Alexandre deployed his dimples and adopted a conspiratorial air, like someone letting you in on a delicious secret, and in the months that followed, the heir became, thanks to the sacred word of his distant friend, a contented exile, without a single link to France left except his amiable business partner.

" . . . that's what I've heard, anyway," Gabriel finished.

He'd told them everything. Alexandre's return, New Zealand, the faraway friend. The money. Everything.

Émilienne was watching him keenly. Gabriel seemed feverish. With a sort of eagerness mixed with fear and excitement, he kept piling on details about the heir, the house, the garden full of heirloom-variety rosebushes, "really amazing ones." Louis shook his head, consumed by curiosity.

"But, so then why come back now?" the farmhand grumbled. "Why doesn't he go back to New Zealand instead of playing the big shot here?"

Gabriel darted a glance at Blanche. She was listening. She hadn't moved.

"She told me he was planning to move back here, but nothing's definite. His parents haven't seen him in twelve years. They're as excited as kids," he mumbled, trying to meet his sister's gaze, which was now fixed unseeingly on the knots in the wooden table, a swarm of unspoken questions visible in her eyes.

"Who is 'she'?"

"Aurore, from Le Marché. Her dad works at the train station with Alexandre's father. He told him everything."

Louis chuckled.

"Oh yes, I'd forgotten about her."

Gabriel shrugged. Émilienne turned away on creaking joints and began running water into the sink full of dirty dishes.

Aurore and Gabriel. *It has a nice ring to it, actually*, thought Blanche, still gazing at the table, at the grooves and ridges in the wood, wishing they would open wide and swallow her, take her down, down, to the center of the earth, beneath these fields and these cows' asses and these chicken feet, beneath Sombre-Étang, where Alexandre's presence still hovered like a spring bird no one was waiting for anymore.

The little house, sandwiched between two others that looked exactly like it, down to the color of the shutters and the length of the grass in the front lawn—the little house made Alexandre shudder as he parked, the wheels of his car exactly parallel to the low wall where an empty brown terracotta vase sat next to a mailbox on which his parents' last name was slowly fading. They never bothered to change the label; the postman knew who lived here: these people, this couple whose son had gotten the hell out of town the moment he reached adulthood, hadn't budged an inch; their lives had not changed, except for the departure of their child for the big city, where people said he'd made a success of himself, had even gone to New Zealand. Their Alexandre, so handsome, so polite, so confident—in New Zealand!

He pushed open the iron gate, his gaze sweeping quickly over the immaculately trimmed lawn, and made his way toward the front door. He hadn't even had time to ring the bell before his mother opened the door, smoothing her blouse, tugging it down, and when she took him in her arms, Alexandre shivered. Childhood rose up in him again like a corpse floating to the surface of a river.

"Well, come in, come in! Don't just stand there!"

He gave her what he thought of as his most charming smile.

After he'd left, the son never went back to his parents' house again. He did call them, and his mother came to visit him several times in the small, tidy room he rented, which he paid for by working weekends and holidays. His father always picked up when he called from his office telephone every Friday afternoon to tell them about his week and ask about theirs. Always the same stories. Alexandre called, and he worried, but he didn't come back. At Christmas and the New Year, he stayed in the city and took holiday work while everyone else traveled or went home to their families. He manned the cash register at the movie theatre, cleared out shelves at the grocery store, it didn't much matter what; he was earning a living. "Mama, it takes money to rent a real apartment, and I have to earn that money somewhere; it's not just going to fall out of the sky," he'd say when his mother begged him to come home, at least for a weekend, Sunday lunch with his family.

On the day his father, from the depths of his armchair, had listened to Alexandre announce over the phone, "I'm coming back to the village. I'll be there on Sunday," the parents had thought something terrible had happened. He'd lost his job, maybe, or developed some terminal disease. They understood neither this return or the self-assured voice on the other end of the line.

Now, going down the narrow hallway, the closed door of his old bedroom beckoning, brimming with memories, Alexandre was overcome by a wave of dizziness. He veered off toward the dining room, where the table stood between the fireplace and the sideboard, set with its china plates painted with blue-and-white country scenes. His mother had cooked roast beef, his father brought out a suitable bottle of red wine. On the other side of the room, out the window, the field bordering the forest had been fenced off, but a two-meter-wide bed of nasturtiums ran along the foot of the fence.

"Those flowers are pretty," he managed to say, sitting down in his place next to his father.

A wide smile lit up his mother's face.

"Aren't they? The owner of the field let us plant them, as long as they didn't take up too much space. Gives a bit of color."

"And it keeps your mother busy," quipped his father.

Alexandre felt suddenly nauseated.

"Are you all right, son? You're not sick, are you?"

The man put a hand on his son's shoulder.

"It's nothing. The emotion of being back," lied Alexandre. Under the table, his foot tapped feverishly on the carpet.

"I'd like to buy that field," he said. "We could put in a ter-race behind the house. Plant more flowers. It would be beauti-ful."

"Oh, you, always with your crazy ideas!" his mother exclaimed, filling her son's plate.

Alexandre shot her a look of fury before restraining himself. For a split second, it was as if a veil of rage covered his face and he was peering through a sort of meshwork, seeing his parents as nothing but bent, blurred silhouettes.

"It's not a crazy idea. I'd like to come back and live around here, make things nice, you know."

They stared at him, dumbfounded.

"But, dear, what on earth would we do with a terrace?" his mother asked, bending over him. "They're nothing but a hassle."

"And wood warps in the rain," his father agreed, taking a sip of wine. "Now eat up before it gets cold, son. You've lost weight; you're working too much, not eating enough."

Alexandre opened his mouth to respond, but his father was hunched over his plate, cutting his meat so forcefully that the entire table shook.

At the end of the meal, they sat for a long while in silence. His mother asked the occasional question about his employer; Alexandre replied that everything was fine, since his return from New Zealand he'd been seen as the team leader. Everything was just fine, really. Nothing much to tell.

"Is there a girl in the picture?" his father asked, as his mother began to clear away the dishes.

Alexandre flinched.

"You really think I have time for that?"

"The Émard girl doesn't have time for it either, I hear."

An image of Blanche's face, against the pillow, flashed through Alexandre's mind.

"I'd like to move back here, start a business, open my own office."

"But why?" his mother called from the kitchen, over the gurgling sound of the coffee pot.

Alexandre sighed, his guts contracting again.

"Because I want to do things properly; I want to have something that belongs just to me."

And then he added:

"And to make you proud of me."

In front of the house, his car, clean, neatly parked, clashed with the gray of the asphalt and the dingy white of the fence. In the middle of the tiny front lawn, hands on his hips, Alexandre gasped for breath. His shoes were getting wet; the hems of his immaculate jeans, wicking up water from the soaked grass, dampened his socks. He'd tugged on his shirt too much; it was wrinkled around his belly button, the shoulders sagging a bit. The cheap synthetic fabric rasped against his skin. He closed his eyes for a long moment, then, very calm, walked to the low wall. He picked up the terra-cotta vase and threw it as hard as he could on the pavement, where it smashed.

Aurore was dozing on Gabriel's bed.

She worked at Le Marché, the café in the square where, every Thursday and the first Sunday of each month, people set up tables, trestles, crates, bags, and tarps. Always selling. More and more. Faster and faster. Aurore understood that; her bosses demanded efficiency from her, especially on market days, saying things like, "The customers should feel like you know what they want even before they order it," and, "Don't give them enough time to start wondering if they've wasted their lives between the moment you take their order and the moment you set a full plate down in front of them." So, she worked quickly.

They'd met in the back room of Le Marché. Gabriel was washing dishes. At first, he'd hardly been able to keep up; she'd shown him a few little time-saving tricks. They'd spent months together in that white kitchen, every day, bright white against the gray weather outside, sparkling clean in the morning and gleaming with grease in the evening, mocking the boss's orders and the customers' drunken guffaws. On the day Gabriel had saved enough money to move across the road he'd walked out of that kitchen, vowing never to come back, and when he'd reached Paradise, his hands red and raw from dish soap, he'd found a cardboard coaster in his jacket pocket, folded in half, with a telephone number written on it and the note "not after ten o'clock."

Gabriel had called. They'd met the next morning. Aurore was wearing her uniform, but, for the first time outside that blasted kitchen, neither of them knew what to say. Gabriel kept his head down, nodding nervously, while Aurore stood beside him, more nervous than she'd been at her first communion. They'd walked a little way through the village's main street, silent and shy and happy, and then they'd returned to their starting point in front of Le Marché, and Gabriel had whispered, "See you tomorrow."

He'd come back the next day. She was wearing her uniform. They'd walked for a little longer this time, and Aurora had said knowingly, smiling, "It's nice just to walk when nothing needs to be said." Every day, they'd played out the same scene, at the same time. Aurore was funny; she made him laugh, and the more this overgrown little boy laughed, the more that laughter was filled with love and joy. Six months of walking and laughter eventually had their effect on Gabriel, and as they were parting one morning, he asked her if they could see each other "in the evening, maybe." He'd stammered a little, adding, "We could walk, or do something else," and Aurore had replied, "I'm sure we'll do something else."

Gabriel's bed was like Gabriel himself: messy, but comfortable. Now that she was in the habit of spending her nights there, Aurore realized that she wouldn't be able to heal Gabriel, that a sort of black tree had taken root inside him in early childhood, a tree watered with fury by his parents' deaths. She couldn't cut it down, only lop off a few boughs when they became too heavy. She cared for the tree, caressed it with her words and her smile, shook it so that the dead leaves and poisoned fruit fell from his soul.

"Aurore?"

She grunted. The day had been a long one. Her clothes still smelled like onion and boiled potato.

"Why has Alexandre come back?"

She raised herself up on an elbow, eyes half-closed, the folds in the sheet imprinted on her cheek.

"Aurore, what do you know about him?"

She pulled herself into a sitting position, crossing her legs. Gabriel had perched on the side of the bed.

"I told you everything my dad told me," she sighed. "Alexandre made a fortune in New Zealand. His parents are very proud."

Gabriel's gaze was fixed on her mouth, searching the movements of her lips for a word she refused to say aloud.

"I just want to try to understand why."

"Why what?"

"Why he came back."

Aurore leaned back against the pillow.

"His father says he's going to buy the land behind their house; he's going to buy the whole village . . . "

Gabriel pictured the horrible little street where Alexandre's parents lived. The hectares of land behind it.

"What's he going to do with it?"

She leaped out of bed, lightly.

"I can't stand this onion smell anymore."

Aurore came around the bed and knelt down in front of Gabriel.

"I really don't know anything about it, Gabriel. I don't know Alexandre. I don't know why he came back."

Then, before he could say a word, she pressed a finger to his lips.

"You're worried for your sister. But there's nothing you can do."

HIDING

B lanche hadn't gone into the attic at Paradise since she was a child. Even back then, she'd been reluctant to set foot in the room, with its menacing beams like frowning eyebrows above her head.

It was a long space crammed with broken furniture and objects of all descriptions that Émilienne had never bothered to throw away. Three-legged tables and chairs; moth-eaten, musty old bed linens, empty picture frames, stacks of large wooden trunks full of old dishes and pots and jugs, draped in tattered blankets. Émilienne kept them "just in case," or maybe she'd simply forgotten everything she'd stored away up here. An armoire with a broken glass front leaned against the wall, full of dresses and sweaters on hangers that Marianne and Étienne had worn in their youth, dresses and sweaters no one would have dared to put on today, so dark were their colors, and their portents.

Blanche had no interest in her mother's things. Briskly, she moved aside boxes of crockery, shook out blankets. A spider alighted gently on her shoulder, as if it didn't want to disturb her, and Blanche dragged another trunk from behind a heavy old dresser missing its drawers. The letter *E* was etched on its lid. She stroked it with a fingertip as if it were a case containing some precious piece of jewelry, and then the spider appeared on its edge.

Mere centimeters away from the creature, Blanche's hand trembled. She wasn't afraid, not of its eight "knitting needles" or the hair that covered them, or the speed with which the tiny animal appeared and disappeared—and yet her hand shook harder and harder, seized with an unexpected convulsion. Blanche leaned closer to the spider, and instead of blowing it away or dislodging it gently, the Émards' daughter picked up the creature, her fingers closing over the round, struggling body. She could feel it against her palm, its legs kicking against this trap in which it suddenly found itself. The quivering of the spider ran through her own body, and her eyelids fluttered slightly before she seemed to come back to herself. She brought her hand to her mouth, the tiny legs stiffening one last time between her lips before being chewed up furiously, like an unripe berry. Blanche kept her eyes open the whole time she was devouring the creature.

She swallowed and stood up and climbed back down through the trap door, her treasure held beneath her left arm, her right hand gripping the rungs of the ladder.

Émilienne always said that Étienne had felt as if he'd moved to a different country when he came to Paradise. His training in geography had given him a fondness for the land. When he wasn't working, Étienne had roamed the Bas-Champs, kneeling beside the water, exploring the trails, parting the dense leaves of the box hedges and clambering through them. When he'd died, his mother-in-law had packed away his things in this box, "just in case," she'd said, "just in case" his children wanted, one day, to know what their father had loved, what passions had made his face light up when he wasn't in the classroom at the school, children buzzing around his tall body like a swarm of bees.

Blanche lifted the lid. Inside, a broken pencil case. A watch, stopped. A photo album, which Blanche knew well because Émilienne had shown them pictures of their parents every day for months, so that the children—especially Gabriel—wouldn't forget them. Gradually, Blanche and her brother had stopped finding any comfort in the images.

*

Notebooks. Of varying sizes. Small sketchbooks. Blue. Inside there were stories, countless stories, some highly detailed; others stopping midsentence. Drawings, maps of Paradise with its little dirt path, the yard sketched quickly, the house to the right with its striped shutters on the windows, the barn to the left, stuffed with hay. Then the domain of the chickens, and behind it all the Bas-Champs and Sombre-Étang. Other notebooks, three of them; larger, with hard covers; no grids inside, only wide black lines. Blanche took one of them from the stack in the bottom of the trunk and leafed gently through its pages, afraid the paper might crumble at her touch.

On the first page, Étienne had written, in his beautiful teacher's handwriting:

A brief history of Paradise

Blanche smiled.

The first volume was a mixture of observations, notes, and sketches. Étienne had inspected each building, each space on the farm; he described the shape of the roof, the cows' muzzles, the sounds the chickens made. He talked about the color of the grass on the other side of the house, and about the pigpen, which frightened him a little.

She spent hours examining the three notebooks. Everything was there. Each volume dealt with a specific subject: the rocks, the animals, the plants. The third book held a faded photograph that showed two naked children in a washtub, a dog's nose poking above their heads. Blanche recognized the bath; it was in the attic now, under the armoire full of sweaters and dresses. Her heart clenched, suddenly assailed by the memory of that afternoon, her mother bathing them outside in that tub. The dog had loped over, wagging its tail, and Gabriel had laughed. She stifled a sob and turned to the next page, where her father had drawn a rough sketch of the pond Émilienne owned some six hundred meters from the farm, behind the slope on which the henhouse perched. The pond was surrounded by thick grass where the cows grazed placidly for a good part of the year. Woods edged the property to the north. Blanche and Gabriel had played at the pond's edge in the summers. Étienne had loved the little body of water; he spent five or six pages describing the curve of its banks, the depth at its center. A brief article cut from the local newspaper had been taped to the inside cover of the notebook, entitled "A little corner of Paradise," and Blanche drew in a deep breath, soaking in her father's penciled words, the secrets they revealed about this man she was sure she had loved. Her father. Louis, Alexandre. They were the only men she'd ever known. One had left her very early, and sometimes she couldn't exactly remember his face. The other lived alongside her like an animal she had to constantly restrain from launching himself at things and people. And the third, Alexandre, had ripped her heart apart the way you tear the paper from a first birthday present.

Whenever Blanche thought back to that last evening, that dinner when her grandmother had held her back against the stone, which had seeped into her back—or maybe it was her body that had sunk into the stone, begging it to swallow her up—when Blanche thought back to the knives slicing through her, she felt Alexandre's presence. She saw Émilienne again, bent over her in the bath; Blanche had been seventeen, almost eighteen, and her grandmother was bathing her and talking to her and holding her as if she were a baby. Her love for Alexandre had stripped her of all her weapons, or maybe she had given them up willingly, out of love for him. She had allowed herself to be seen as she really was, so young, so light, relieved of everything that had been weighing her down, and he had broken her. It had been his apologetic air, even more than his leaving; that stupid ambition of his, when she and Louis got up so early and worked so hard for Paradise—yes, that's what was devastating her now, all over again: Alexandre's words, those pathetic words he couldn't do anything with except string them together to form pretty sentences without any depth or meaning. And she, broken-hearted, crumpled against her grandmother, who had fought so that she wouldn't fall, who had always fought, so that Blanche would be strong.

Since she had learned the news, learned that Alexandre was hanging around town again, just a few kilometers from Paradise, Blanche hadn't set foot beyond the boundaries of their own property. Louis took care of things at the market on

Thursdays and the first Sunday of each month; he didn't ask questions, just carried out Émilienne's silent orders. Blanche crossed the yard and went down to the pigpen and then came back, inspecting the barn and feeding the chickens. She was in constant motion, unable to sit still, terrified. Émilienne watched her through the kitchen window and said nothing.

Alexandre was back.

It was all people were talking about, at Le Marché, in the village, at church.

Protected by the stockades of Paradise, Blanche prepared herself—for what, she wasn't sure, but she prepared herself. Her body was tense, rigid, as if a tree limb were growing inside her; she moved like a machine, so straight, so precise, with such dreadful, cold energy, and rumination, and tightly controlled rage. Alexandre was back, and he hadn't told anyone he was coming, hadn't announced anything in the village; no, he was simply here, alive and well, back home, in the place he had hated. Blanche was preparing herself to accept his presence near her, to accept that it was enough for her to go to the village to cross paths with him, to hear his voice, his name. Alexandre.

Thirty years old. What had she accomplished? What had happened in her life since that disastrous night?

"So little," she murmured aloud, her eyes closed. So little.

The past twelve years had been grueling. And so beautiful. Each morning, the sight of the yard and the scarlet tree flooded her heart with hope, crushing the rage that Alexandre's departure had fueled in her. Each evening, the sky hanging low over the pond, the cowbells chiming from the stable, brought a comfort she couldn't quite describe. The routine sounds, the familiar colors made it possible for her to go to bed, to drift into a sleep where her dreams looked very much like everyday life. Blanche had learned everything about the land, the animals she raised in order to kill, the other farmers, whom she distrusted even as she worked alongside them. She had learned to be solid, respectable. But Alexandre, with his big ideas, his big dreams, and his little words, had swayed her. No one else had ever swayed her that way. No one. Of course, boys, and men—and sometimes the fathers of those boys and men—had invited her out. Blanche wasn't stupid; she said yes, and then had Louis drive her to meet them. At the sight of the two approaching together, they invariably forgot the girl, focusing instead on the bogeyman next to her. No one ever discovered that her pubic hair was the same color as the leaves on the tree in the yard.

Hearing Alexandre's name had awoken a beast in her, a creature of desire and tears. Blanche prepared herself; she patrolled Paradise unceasingly. When she stopped, exhausted, she forced herself to go to sleep as quickly as possible, haunted by Alexandre's beautiful, sweet face. That face, which never failed to stir flickering flames inside her.

The village square was an open belly, swarming with men and women, children and animals. Tables were set out beneath awnings, some forty of them in all; children dodged between sellers' legs, sometimes getting scratched up on the edge of a low wall or a stand overflowing with fruit. On Thursday, the square was crammed with people until late in the afternoon, the first vendors arriving to unload at five in the morning, the "livestockers"—so nicknamed because they sold live animals—coming later. Occupying the area in front of the church, their stalls teemed with feathers and fur, grunting and scratching. Children played near the animals, the one who could get closest without receiving a slap on the wrist winning the game. Every week, rain or snow or shine, Thursday was market day.

At her stall, behind her calm façade, Blanche managed the conversations and the till with one eye on the central promenade and the other on the customers browsing through her eggs, her tomatoes, her lettuces, her chickens in a cage they couldn't escape unless hauled out by the scruff. On this Thursday, she was standing in for Louis, detained at the farm by the difficult birth of a calf. Émilienne hadn't needed to nudge her granddaughter; she had naturally volunteered. For the first time since the news of Alexandre's return, she was breaching the borders of her realm, away from her bedroom, her woods, her beloved pigpen where the pigs, wallowing in the mud, snuffling among the scraps tossed to them over the fence, seemed to her better companions than these people acknowledging her with a wave or a quick but polite word, or a gentle tap on her back—she, who hated to be touched. Since Alexandre, the slightest caress opened a bottomless pit inside her; the faintest quiver, even friendly, even welcoming, reawakened the nightmare of abandonment. Only Émilienne and Gabriel were allowed, on rare occasions, to embrace her gently, or brush her hand, or murmur a loving word—but always very softly, to protect her from what smoldered inside her, that nameless ogre, that scaffold of grief and pain, of pride and resignation.

The market was crowded that day. More so than usual. From her stall, Blanche could see the steeple of the church. That long, tall arrow towering over their lives soothed her. She was making change for an old lady who was talking about how she'd known her when she was a little girl, when her parents were still in this world. Blanche wanted to reply that no, her parents weren't the "poor souls" of the story, that the "poor souls" were the ones who remained, all the Émiliennes of the world, and no, she didn't remember the name of this woman chattering away at her. But she held her tongue and handed over the three coins, and the woman went on her way. She was stowing the crumpled bill in their little moneybox when four simple words rose above the buzz of conversation around her:

"Well, there you are."

That voice.

It wasn't a boy's voice anymore. There was still, in that "well," something of the habitual attempt to please, to create the illusion of mutual trust in just a few seconds. That voice came from a distant land; it had been changed by work, by fatigue, by speaking itself; it was a voice used to being listened to, but Blanche recognized in that "well," in that way of ending the sentence, the expectation that the voice would remind her of the gentle boy who had gestured out her bedroom window at the oak tree. Confident in her preparations for this conflict, she looked up, straight into Alexandre's eyes, ready for anything, fortified by the violence of childhood.

That violence had no effect on Alexandre. He simply let it slide off his back, and as his lips curved in a sheepish smile, Blanche, overwhelmed by the sight of his face, remodeled by the years, drank in every line of his features wordlessly. A taller man, and thinner, than the boy she had known, was looking at her now with bewildering tenderness. Blanche had to turn her head, to look away. Alexandre wore a button-down shirt and dark trousers. She had never seen him dressed so casually. Now he waited, so calm, so sure of himself, for her to speak at last.

"I'm really the one who should be saying that to you, '*Well, there you are.*'"

Her voice was hard.

"That's true," he acknowledged, his smile widening even further.

Behind him, two customers were waiting. Blanche shot him a dark glance and refilled the egg baskets, mechanically. Alexandre stood, his spine very straight, one hand on the table and the other in the back pocket of his trousers, his eyes moving from Blanche to the customers, giving them his best "you won't regret your decision to buy these" look. When they left the stall, she beckoned him closer, as if to tell him a secret.

"You don't need to do that," she whispered, forbiddingly.

"Do what?"

Exasperated, she gestured at the customers, now on the other side of the street.

"What you just did, there. I can manage perfectly well. We haven't just been waiting around for you."

Alexandre took a step back.

"Yes, I can see that. Congratulations on Paradise."

"Did you think we wouldn't make it?"

He looked away and said, his voice almost boyish:

"I never doubted you. Best of luck with your work, Blanche."

He gave her a little wave of farewell and vanished into the crowd gathered in front of the church. Two more customers approached the stall just then; Blanche left them by the chicken cage, turned her back, and leaned against the stack of crates. Bent double. Overcome.

DRYING

Louis wiped the clean soup plates dry as Émilienne handed them to him. Doing the dishes, taking out the garbage, dusting the table, sweeping the floor—he enjoyed these moments. Side by side, at this sink chipped in its corner by thousands of uses, meals, large feasts, he felt close to Émilienne. This interlude lasted only a few minutes, but it might as well have been hours, so deeply did he feel like he belonged, like he was part of the family. When Émilienne made the familiar gesture with the plate, lifting it out of the water, shaking it briefly between two capable fingers and flipping it over, a movement her old hands performed as naturally as breathing, Louis felt as if he was receiving all her confidence, her trust that he wouldn't break this plate, or the equilibrium of Paradise.

"Have you seen him yet?" Émilienne asked.

"No."

He wiped his hands with the damp dishtowel.

"Wait, here, use this one," she said, plucking a dry cloth from the shelf with her wet fingertips.

She drew in a deep breath.

"Are you planning on going to see him?"

It hadn't occurred to him, not for a single second. Seeing Alexandre would mean seeing Blanche, that night, her face twisted with pain. The memory was unbearable.

"No, I hadn't planned on it."

Émilienne sniffed.

"But I will, if you ask me to," he added, quickly.

She pulled the plug from the sink's drain, the murky water disappearing with a gurgle.

"I'm not asking you to do anything, Louis."

He stood next to her, the docile manservant. The dishes were done. He was Émilienne's employee again. He started for the small door that opened onto the back of the yard, where Émilienne tossed vegetable peelings and eggshells, but she stopped him, asking, her voice quivering:

"Do you think he came back for her?"

The farmhand wanted to touch Émilienne's arm reassuringly, but he didn't feel like he could do it. He looked closely at her face. She had aged. Her eyes were vanishing into the mass of wrinkles that was engulfing them like an insatiable, ever-rising river. The green of those time-swallowed eyes, so hard, so beautiful, was fading to gray, the gray of earth, of a mare's coat, a gray that tarnished everything, amplifying small fears, trivial worries.

"He won't be nasty," he whispered, backing up a step, toward the door. "I'll make sure of it."

Émilienne draped the wet dishtowel over the edge of the sink and murmured:

"That won't change anything. She loves him."

Louis spent the rest of the day lost in thought. He felt as if he were at the center of a maze whose pathways were constantly being redrawn. He had followed the same route so many times, skipped from one event to another, exhausted himself trying to understand, focusing his memory, his passion for Blanche, coming up with strategies to get rid of Alexandre, to drive him away. Then he remembered that Alexandre, too, had been born here; that his parents lived here, just a few kilometers away, and that no one had the right to control this young man's life. And so, there was nothing he could say, nothing he could do, nothing except keep an eye on Blanche. He would never reach out a hand to her or ask her to touch him.

Alexandre was back.

For twelve years, Louis had endeavored to be the man of Paradise, reduced to his discretion and his duties, defined by his usefulness. Louis had a room of his own now; he didn't have to be careful about the light or the noise anymore or lock the door when he pleasured himself with his right hand. He didn't have to wait hours for the bathroom anymore while Gabriel spent a ridiculous amount of time soaking in the tub, *completely still*, Louis had always noticed, even as he hammered on the door. Gabriel had never even touched himself back then; his mind was on other things that Louis couldn't comprehend. Now the bathroom was almost always free, the hallway almost always empty, and the bedroom enormous. At the other end of the house, in the big bed where Louis dreamed of joining her, Blanche was thinking of the Bas-Champs. He was sure of it; for twelve years it was all she'd ever talked about, the land; Sombre-Étang; the little ring of dark forest, and the "chemins des dames," or ladies' paths, as Émilienne called the little dried-up streambeds that connected the neighboring farms to one another. Blanche was always calculating the price per hectare of land in ten years' time, or reading up, she said, on new machines for milking, harvesting, managing livestock. They had to prepare themselves already for competition, for unparalleled cruelty, modern, consuming, indifferent; competition was signaling its presence in rural areas, and there was talk about the distress of country farmers, of suicides, unpaid bills, dreadful isolation. Émilienne, in her armchair, murmured, "I won't be here to see it, but you . . . " and it weighed on Blanche's mind. She had opened another bank account, where she squirreled away what she could, enough to borrow on in a few years' time. She had plans to renovate some of the outbuildings next to the barn, to enlarge the pigpen. Louis never offered his opinion, and no one asked him for it.

Since Alexandre's return, Blanche spoke even less. Still dreaming, maybe. Louis sensed the heaviness weighing on her, but saying Alexandre's name would have made him *present*. The wound was open, throbbing in Blanche's memory, and it would be her decision alone to close it once and for all. Louis could only be there, a sentry in the shadows.

One late afternoon, exhausted by his own ruminations, he went to Le Marché on foot. Aurore was waiting tables. He waved discreetly in greeting and she came over, touching his shoulder lightly in a friendly gesture, and showed him to a table. The leather of the bench seat cradled him comfortably, and he had to fight not to fall asleep. Without his even asking, Aurore brought him a pint of beer. He drank half of it down thirstily, its bitter savor giving him new energy. Again, he imagined what Blanche must be going through, wondered how she managed to sleep at night. Did she cry every day? Did she, too, touch herself to help bring sleep? Louis hunched over the table like a child at the back of a class, rested his head on his folded arms, and closed his eyes. From a distance, it looked as if he were weeping, but he was simply retreating into himself, looking for Blanche.

A conversation among three men at the bar brought him out of his reverie. Two of them were talking very loudly. The workday was over; they were feeling good, and they wanted everyone to know it. They ordered beers—"lots of beers"—added the oldest of the three—and the quietest one murmured, "These are on me." A king buying a round. His curiosity piqued, Louis glanced over at the intruders and recognized Alexandre.

Louis shifted slightly to the left, pressing himself against the wall. The men didn't see him. He scrutinized the trio. They were standing at the bar. The man who had ordered was thanking Alexandre, thumping him on the back, and Louis saw the young man shrug. A beer or two, or even three, was nothing to him. He earned good money; he could afford to play the lord with his modest shrugs.

The other two were cuffing him playfully on the back of the neck, roaring, "Back in the fold, eh, little Alexandre?" and Alexandre replied, "I'm not so little anymore, and I've got ideas." Now they were howling with laughter, repeating, "Ideas, always ideas!" Alexandre ordered another round of drinks without waiting for them to finish the ones they had, and Louis, from his booth, watched him do it. After a moment, the first man knocked on the bar three times and shook his companions' hands, claiming that "Madame was waiting at home." When he had gone, Alexandre pulled up a stool and rested a hip against it without sitting down fully. A silence fell between the remaining two men, and then the one who had laughed so hard a few minutes ago spat:

"Goddamned women, eh?"

Louis pricked up his ears.

Alexandre was gazing at the rows of bottles behind the bar as if he were alone and his companion had already left. Louis chose that moment to rise, squeezing between two tables. Surprised, the two men turned. When he recognized him, Alexandre showed so little surprise that Louis was almost disappointed. He continued toward the bathroom, and Alexandre nodded slightly in greeting.

Louis splashed his hands and face with water that smelled of cheap soap and emerged from the bathroom slightly less pale, passing the last two customers left in the bar to toss a bill on his table. Just as he was about to step outside into the fresh air, he heard Alexandre say very distinctly:

"It's better when they're submissive."

Aurore hadn't even had time to call out a farewell. Louis turned back on the threshold of the heavy glass door flanked by posters and advertisements. His body was quivering.

"Repeat what you just said."

Alexandre's face took on that apologetic air that Louis hated, the same look he'd had that last evening in Paradise.

"I don't know what you're talking about."

Next to him, his companion smirked drunkenly. He opened his mouth to speak but managed only a sonorous belch. Alexandre wanted to laugh but didn't get the chance. Suddenly, Louis was very close to him. Alexandre could smell his breath, the scent of beer filling his nostrils.

"Louis, I swear, I don't know what you're talk—"

The impact sent him sprawling against bar. The farmhand had struck him at the corner of the eye, where it hurts, where it makes your vision and your mind go blurry. Alexandre doubled over, covering his head with his hand to protect himself. Louis grabbed him by the back of the neck and smashed a fist into his nose, bringing forth a gush of bright red blood. Alexandre cried out and his companion scuttled to the far end of the bar, stammering unintelligibly, while Aurore waited behind the bar for the scuffle to end, a bored expression on her face.

Alexandre was on his knees, both hands pressed to his nose. His shirt, spotted with pink snot and sweat, stuck to his ribs and his torso. Louis stood over him, shifting from foot to foot like a boxer, hissing, "Get up, come on, get up." But Alexandre didn't move, and when Louis gave him a heavy kick in the stomach, he crumpled, defeated, and lost consciousness.

Helping

Alexandre could barely walk. He could feel his face throbbing. He moved slowly down the upstairs hallway, Blanche's arm around his neck. Beneath the acrid odor of sweat, she could smell his fragrance, the scent of his skin. Aurore supported him from the other side, gripping his hand, his arm over her shoulders. The young man groaned. Pain lanced through him, as if an army were shooting him with long, tiny arrows.

Aurore opened the bedroom door and the two women helped Alexandre sit down. His mouth twisted when Blanche inspected his wounds. Louis had hit him hard. Nothing could be seen of the boyish face but an enormously swollen nose, two puffy eyelids impossible to lift, and a pair of tear-filled eyes in which Blanche could read all of Alexandre's surprise, all of his recognition. The young woman ran to the bathroom and rummaged in the small cupboard beneath the sink, extracting compresses, a bottle of rubbing alcohol, and a spray bottle she filled with ice water. When she came back, he was drowsing, held upright in Aurore's arms, half-conscious. Blanche sprayed his face with cold water three times and pressed the compress to his nose. He let out a gasp.

"You're as much of a sissy as you always were," she murmured, tossing aside his makeshift dressing.

Alexandre tried to smile, but moving his lips only intensified the pain. Blanche spritzed his face with cold water again.

"You're going to be quite a sight for the next ten days or so," she said, proudly.

Aurore stifled a laugh. He let himself fall back on the mattress, curling himself into the fetal position. Blanche studied his face closely, and when he tried to untuck the sheets to slide between them, Aurore hurried to help him, unbuttoning his shirt while he sank into the pillows—*still the same ones as on butchering day*, thought Blanche. Before closing the door softly behind her, she paused for a moment, seized with the desire to look at him, one more time, in the bed they had once shared.

"What's he doing here?" growled Louis, from the bottom of the staircase.

Aurore went past him and vanished into the kitchen. Blanche descended the stairs, her face impassive, and when she tried to leave, Louis got between her and the door. Anger distorted his features, his nostrils flaring. Blanche looked him straight in the eye.

"Would you rather we took him home to his parents' house in this condition? Or put him to bed in your room?"

"*Anywhere* else!"

"You should have thought of that before," she said, her voice firm.

Émilienne's voice. Blanche was so much like her. He sat down on the bottom step.

"It was for you," he whispered.

"Stop."

He looked up and saw Blanche standing over him, her lips pressed into a thin line.

"He said something horrible."

"I don't want to know," she said, turning away toward the door and seizing the knob.

"He said he preferred submissive women, that it's easier with them."

Blanche let out a hiccup of surprise. Aurore came out of the dining room and saw Louis sitting in front of the open door. She opened her mouth to say something, but he gestured for her to go.

When she had disappeared in her turn, he hesitated for a few seconds and then left the house. He went quickly across the yard, calling after Aurore.

"I'll come and sleep at Gabriel's."

They set off together, silently, into the night.

Alexandre was at the table with yesterday's newspaper. It had been a long night. Blanche's face, drawn with fatigue, sweating with fury at Louis. The wounds on Alexandre's battered face had stopped seeping. He sat lopsidedly, his left eye forced open with difficulty, leafing through the paper, his body twisted, a steaming cup of hot coffee in front of him atop a dishtowel folded in quarters.

"I made coffee."

Another full cup was waiting for Blanche, covered with a saucer.

"To keep it warm," he explained.

Blanche let out a breath. She was desperate for the coffee, but not coffee made by Alexandre here, in her home, in the place where they had parted ways.

"Where is Louis?"

Blanche's voice was hoarse.

"He didn't sleep here."

She shrugged.

"Is Émilienne out with the chickens?" she asked, going to the window.

The yard rustled in the morning breeze. It was going to be a beautiful day.

"I haven't seen her," said Alexandre.

Blanche whipped around.

"What?"

"I haven't seen her this morning. She must still be sleeping."

She glanced at the clock above the sink. Eight-fifteen. Émilienne was always up by seven.

She ran for the front hall, took the stairs four at a time, and flung Émilienne's door open frantically. Her grandmother sat at the foot of the bed, one hand pressed to her stomach, the other clenched, dripping, on the sheets. Her lips, eyes, cheeks were horribly pale.

"Can you stand up?"

Émilienne nodded, very slowly.

"Your stomach?"

Another nod.

"Don't move. I'll call a doctor."

She turned and nearly collided with Alexandre.

"We have to take her," he whispered. "We have to take her straight to the hospital, right now."

Blanche hesitated.

"Look at her; if you wait for the doctor on call, he'll tell you the same thing. We'll have wasted time. Do you have a car?"

"It's parked a little way off."

"I know someone at the hospital in the city. They'll treat her as a priority, you have my word."

Blanche couldn't make a decision. Émilienne would suffer martyrdom before she uttered a single complaint.

"Who'll look after the animals?"

Alexandre rolled his eyes.

"Louis will come back. He can be here by himself for a day."

Blanche heard her grandmother gasp for breath. She gestured for Alexandre to help her, and the two of them lifted the old woman and maneuvered her down the stairs. The journey from her bedroom to the front hall seemed to take hours. When they were finally at the door, Blanche sped off to get her car and pulled it around to the bottom of the porch steps. They put Émilienne in the back seat, leaning against the passenger-side door, legs stretched out.

"I'll drive," said Alexandre.

"You can only see out of one eye."

"That's plenty. I know where I'm going; it'll save time."

Alexandre drove quickly, but carefully. Blanche, in the passenger seat, kept casting frequent, anxious glances at her grandmother. Émilienne clutched her stomach with both hands, her face drawn, lips pressed tightly together. *She's suffering*, thought Blanche. *She's suffering, and I can't do anything to stop it.*

"Faster!"

The engine roared.

They reached the emergency entrance thirty minutes later. Alexandre got out first; he disappeared between the sliding doors, and Blanche heard him shouting, "We need help!" He reemerged with two orderlies beside him, tall and sturdy. They took Émilienne inside. Alexandre walked behind Blanche down the hall, where other sick patients were waiting. A nurse asked them if they wanted to wait, but Alexandre asked to see Doctor Neyrie. Raising her eyebrows slightly at the sound of the name, she ushered Blanche and Alexandre into a small adjoining room, where Blanche crumpled into a chair.

"She'll be all right," said Alexandre, very gently.

"Of course she will."

He came closer to Blanche. She flinched.

"I know Doctor Neyrie. My company sold his house when he divorced his wife; I'm the one who took care of everything."

"Including his wife?"

Alexandre paled. He moved away into a corner of the room. She didn't look at him, uninterested in his presence.

After a long moment, a man came into the room. Blanche leapt to her feet. Alexandre, in his corner, stepped forward cautiously.

"Mademoiselle Émard?"

Blanche nodded wordlessly.

"It's a bowel obstruction. You did well to get her here so quickly. We'll need to keep her here for a few days."

He turned, and a wide smile lit up his face, which had been so serious when giving his diagnosis.

"Alexandre! How good to see you! How are you? What on earth's happened to your face?!"

They shook hands warmly.

"Fine, I'm fine," Alexandre stammered. "Don't worry about me."

The doctor clapped him on the shoulder. "You did the right thing."

He turned to Blanche. "She needs to rest. We'll keep her at least for this week. But it'll take some time. At her age, you know how these things can be."

He left the small room with a last wave to Alexandre. Things began to blur together in Blanche's head: Émilienne's face, her silence, Alexandre at the wheel of the car, so sure of himself, so anxious, too, and this doctor who spoke to him as if he were his own son. Blanche felt as if she'd shifted into another dimension, symbols and images and warnings swirling around her, overwhelming her exhausted brain.

"Get some rest, Blanche."

Alexandre's voice seemed to come from a long way off.

"Blanche?"

He'd put his hand on her arm to get her attention. They hadn't been so near one another since his return. From this close up, his bruised and swollen face was truly ghastly.

"God, you're hideous," she said.

Alexandre smiled briefly.

"It's very trendy right now, cockfighting."

Blanche stood up with difficulty and vanished into the hall without slamming the door behind her, and in that simple, restrained gesture, Alexandre sensed the beginnings, infinitesimal as they were, of renewed trust.

Tending

T he house was empty.

And yet, the floorboards creaked, the roof murmured, the beams in the attic groaned. A dormouse could be heard skittering. The frequent barking of the dog, in its place in front of the barn, penetrated the thick walls. When the wind blew hard, the windows rattled like a skeleton. The napkin folded in quarters on the table, the cup still atop it, the coffee left in the cup; the newspaper, open to the real estate listings; another cup, on the table, its bottom stained with a dark ring. The bench seat askew. The coffeepot half-full. Louis studied each object, searched the kitchen and the dining room for some hint, some clue.

He'd woken early, on Blanche's brother's sofa. He'd heard Aurore's breathing in the dimness, lighter and more serene than Gabriel's. For a split second he'd been tempted to go closer, to watch them sleeping so peacefully. Then he had turned and opened the door noiselessly and crossed the street, stoop-shouldered, his forty-year-old bachelor's body in the dawn light like an animal crossing a field of flowers.

His first, reflexive act was to go upstairs. The covers on Blanche's bed were pulled back on one side only. A wave of relief washed over him. They hadn't slept together; Blanche hadn't joined Alexandre in the night. She had undoubtedly taken refuge in Louis's own bedroom with its two twin beds. He glanced inside. She had clearly slept late; he could smell her morning scent, the smell of skin that has spent hours steeping in bed linen, that smell that is only bearable if you love someone.

He'd never known the house to be empty. No note on the table, not a sign of life, simply that square of cloth with the coffee cup on top. Alexandre had had breakfast here, had read the newspaper. Blanche had remained standing, perhaps leaning against the wall where Émilienne had held her that evening. They'd chatted together like an old married couple.

A couple.

The idea tore him apart. He saw them, both of them, there in the kitchen where Louis had rejected his mother in favor of Émilienne; he saw them there, contentedly settled in. His fist clenched the dishtowel. Through the window he saw the chickens gathered in front of the porch steps, their clucking more agitated than usual.

Where was Émilienne?

Louis left the dining room at a run. The grandmother's room was empty. She wasn't there, but the bed hadn't been made, and the covers had been pulled to one side, trailing on the floor. A large sweat stain was visible on the mattress, and Émilienne's glasses sat on the nightstand, neatly folded on top of a book next to a tube of medicine.

He circled the room in a sort of animalistic frenzy. Where were they all? Why hadn't anyone said anything to him? Why was he here, alone, now? An old feeling rose up in him, one from childhood, from those evenings when he had stayed outside on the front step, to keep away from his father's fists. Alone. He went to the window, opened it, drew in a deep breath of the fresh air scented with hay and earth and manure.

He didn't belong to this family. He was an employee here. No one had spoken to him because they didn't expect anything from him except what you would normally expect from a farmhand. Feed the chickens. Clean the yard. Take care of the barn. Sort the eggs. Milk the cows. He wasn't part of the family; he was part of the farm. Louis had forgotten what it meant, to be part of the scenery without being part of the picture.

Before going back downstairs, he stripped the sheets from Émilienne's bed, dropping them in a pile on the floor. *At least she won't have to sleep in a dirty bed when she gets home.*

The car pulled hastily into the yard just as Louis was setting off down the slope toward the pigpen. The crunch of wheels on the beaten earth startled him and he whirled around, shoulders hunched, fists raised. When the driver's side door opened, he expected to see Alexandre step out of the car, but it was Blanche who appeared instead, breathless. Their eyes met, full of inexpressible reproach. Louis moved closer. She was wearing Alexandre's jacket.

"Wow, things are progressing quickly, I see."

"Shut up."

Blanche's voice was low, deep, almost masculine. Émilienne's voice, whenever anything went wrong.

"Émilienne's in the hospital," she said.

"Why didn't you tell me?"

"I called, but you didn't answer," Blanche lied.

I must already have left when she tried to reach me, Louis thought.

"I'll go there now," he said stepping closer. "Give me the keys."

She shied away.

"Alexandre's with her."

Pain lanced through his heart, deep and sharp, like a tree being cut down.

"Why him?" he asked, the words coming out as a groan.

He didn't say anything else. An image of Louis in Marianne and Étienne's bedroom, his face ravaged by his own father's fists, appeared in Blanche's mind, and then Alexandre's face was superimposed on it, in that same room, at that same time of night.

"He knew the doctor, Louis."

She'd pronounced his first name distinctly, impressing each

word on him so he would understand. Alexandre knew the doctor, and so Émilienne had been treated more quickly.

His hands were trembling. They embarrassed him, these hands used to cowhide and dog hair and the rough bark of trees. He didn't know what to do with them, so he scratched at some imaginary sores.

"You should have left a note. I was worried."

Blanche could sense the anger draining from his voice. Louis loved Émilienne as much as she did. She imagined how he must have felt when he came home, with no one in the house or outside. She realized how furious she would have been in his place, with how long he'd been taking care of this family, this Paradise, with how long he'd been reminded, every day, that he would never be part of it.

"There wasn't time . . . you should have seen her, when I found her . . . "

Then she added:

"I asked myself what you would have done, in my place."

Louis sighed. He turned and continued toward the pigpen, pretending to ignore what had just been said.

She watched him disappear down the slope, his big frame swaying among the trees.

F or a week, Blanche and Gabriel took turns at Émilienne's bedside.

She was recovering, but weak. The first time they'd seen her after her arrival at the hospital, they'd been shocked by the pallor of her skin, by the sight of her lying in bed, woozy from drugs. Standing next to their grandmother, they'd hardly moved. Émilienne had gazed back at them between half-shut eyelids. Blanche had spent that first day in a chair next to the bed. When she'd come back to the hospital, Alexandre was waiting at the door of Émilienne's room. "I figured I probably shouldn't go in," he'd stammered, "but the nurses say she's doing well; she's very tired, but she's doing well," and then he'd withdrawn silently, like a manservant.

Aurore accompanied Gabriel to the hospital twice a day, staying in the lobby while he went to the room. Every morning, Alexandre was there. Sitting in a chair, magazine in hand, waiting for Blanche, very well dressed, neatly groomed, at ease, confident yet unobtrusive. When Blanche appeared, he spoke to her briefly, and then left the hospital.

Gabriel always walked through the hospital entrance first. At first, he'd simply waved to Alexandre in greeting. After all, Alexandre knew the doctor; it had been his idea to come directly to the hospital rather than making Émilienne wait. Gabriel knew he owed his grandmother's comfort, and Blanche's relief, to him.

Alexandre's face still bore traces of his fight with Louis. Gabriel figured he'd probably had it coming, really had it coming. To his credit, Alexandre didn't complain, just carried on, with his black eye fading to yellow and the rainbow of bruises on his cheekbones. For a week, they came and went, speaking little, filing past beneath the orderlies' watchful eyes. On the following Monday, Émilienne was taken home in an ambulance. That morning, Blanche looked around for Alexandre despite herself, uneasy at first, then reassuring herself that he must know her grandmother was leaving the hospital.

Back at Paradise, the two ambulance attendants wanted to help Émilienne upstairs, but she refused, protesting that she was perfectly fit to die in her kitchen. Louis, beneath the tree, watched them assisting her up the porch steps. She was skin and bones, like a crumpled sheet of paper. He read in their eyes a kind of admiration for this old lady, but they had absolutely no idea how much she needed this place, the same way she needed water or oxygen. Every hour spent in the hospital, away from Paradise, had weakened her. They helped her sit down at the kitchen table. One of the attendants unfolded a page of instructions, smoothing it with the palm of his hand, repeating that she had to "follow the directions carefully." Émilienne agreed, exasperated; yes, she would take her medication; yes, she'd be very careful; yes, she'd follow the prescribed diet to the letter, and when he told her for the tenth time to "take care of herself," she murmured:

"Please, go now, if you don't mind. I understand everything you've said. I'm old, not deaf."

When the ambulance had departed, Louis unfolded himself from beneath the tree. His big hands, buried in the pockets of his work coveralls, had dug into the fabric so hard as to poke holes in it. He hadn't seen Émilienne in eight days. Walking into the dining room, where Blanche was mulling over which leftovers to prepare for dinner, he felt like a little boy again. He edged over to the window and whispered:

"Hello, Émilienne."

The grandmother nodded at him. Louis had never seen her so glum, so weak.

"Since when do you take vacations without warning me?"

Blanche, Louis, Gabriel, and Aurore worked together to care for Émilienne. Aurore cooked dishes of vegetables and rice and potatoes and prepared jars of stewed fruit, which she stored in a cool place according to the doctor's instructions. Blanche refilled the pill dispenser each night: three tablets, three times a day. She wanted Émilienne to be comfortable, to regain her strength. The operation had weakened her; in the days following her return home, she couldn't manage the stairs to her bedroom alone. Every morning she took one more step in the kitchen or the front hall, on the porch or in the yard; every one of those steps was a victory, and Blanche saw how Louis, so attentive to Émilienne, to the expression on her face when exhaustion took over, went out of his way to encourage her. He supported her, bearing her old woman's weight on his overgrown boy's arm, talking with her about his day, or the cranes that had come back to the pond. Louis brought Émilienne back to a place where she was strong, solid; he compelled her, calmly and gently, to make it to the door, to the gate, to use her mind and her memory in spite of fatigue and old age and the shock of eight days spent in a hospital room. Watching Émilienne make her way through the immense yard, her steps so achingly slow, Blanche feared that the immobile week outside Paradise had sapped her strength forever. Leaving her land had brought the full force of her years crashing down on her. Time had affected her like ice water on delicate lingerie; Émilienne had shriveled with age. Soon, despite everything she had given to this place, she would no longer belong to this earth—or rather, she would belong to it utterly and completely, would be consumed by it.

Blanche sensed that the end was near. Émilienne seemed so agonizingly vulnerable. Her granddaughter had never seen her like this. And Louis was caring for her as if his own life depended on it. Sometimes Blanche thought Émilienne didn't really need her, or Gabriel. That this man was enough, this unexpected protector, on whom she had breathed gently for so long to revive his flame.

For three weeks, neither Blanche nor Louis left Paradise. They tended to Émilienne, while Gabriel managed things at the market with Aurore. Once a week, they set up their tables and trestles, amorous as lovebirds beneath the scandalized, skeptical, and occasionally fond gazes of the market regulars. In truth, Gabriel had never been so alive as he was during those few days, those three consecutive Thursdays when he reigned, finally, over a tiny scrap of Paradise, his queen at his side, whom he loved the way Blanche loved the land and Louis loved Émilienne: unconditionally.

And so, they carried on that way. The days passed, and Émilienne slowly regained the use of her limbs. The further she seemed from danger, the more Blanche's thoughts roved beyond the boundaries of Paradise. She hadn't seen Alexandre since that second-to-last day at the hospital. He had been there every morning, sitting in the waiting room. They'd exchanged a few words about the weather and Émilienne's condition. Then he'd left the building, calmly, and she'd watched him go, every time, always in the same direction.

But since Émilienne's return to Paradise, nothing. Not a call, not a note. Blanche had thought perhaps he was afraid of Louis, that he was taking a step back while Émilienne regained her strength. She'd tried to reassure herself by repeating that he had "other things to do," but after three weeks without a word, she was beginning to feel stripped of her reason, anguish threatening to overwhelm her. She waited, like the wife of a sea captain, for some sign, some news of him. Anything. Some hint.

On the fourth market Thursday, unable to bear it any longer, she begged Gabriel and Aurore to let her go instead, insisting when they balked at the idea that she "needed some air." They looked back at her, certain she was lying. At last they gave in, still offering to go along and help her, which she refused. Blanche wanted to take back the reins of Paradise, and she wanted to do it alone, backed up by Louis, each at their own station, with their own mission, their own animals, their own secrets. Their own actions. And each with their own fears of being merely transient, temporary; of destroying what was already fragile, of spoiling the beauty. Each with their nights of anger, their dawn awakenings, and each for themselves, and all for Émilienne, to the end.

In choosing to live elsewhere, Gabriel and Aurore pushed themselves away from the shores of Paradise, navigating the same waters as Blanche without encountering the same rocky shoals, always retreating, hand in hand, to the little cabin a few hundred meters from Émilienne's house.

It was hot enough to cook the eggs in their shells. Blanche covered them with a damp cloth. Sweat beaded on her forehead, curling the wisps of hair behind her delicate, almost bony ears. The market was crammed to bursting on this first market Thursday in May; a mob of tourists and regulars, merchants and farmers, children and old people pressed close in front of the stalls. People negotiated three for the price of two, shook hands without knowing each other, kissed without loving each other in the shadow of the church bell tower, which chimed every half hour. The vendors cast a quick eye over their accounts; the minutes ticked by, and the money flowed in. The spring was dying rapidly, smothered by the damp heat of what promised to be a scorching summer.

Blanche hadn't appeared in public since Émilienne's hospitalization. People kept coming over to see her, hugging her tightly and asking for news, always requesting more details, making more assumptions, buying more eggs from her than usual, mentioning Gabriel and his "pretty girl . . . ." No one could ever remember her name. "Aurore," Blanche said, sighing, "it's Aurore," but they kept referring to her as "that pretty girl." By the end of the morning, her stock was almost completely sold out, one sale immediately following another, and the conversations too, and in that uninterrupted flow of faces, customers, regulars, no trace of Alexandre.

The bells were chiming twelve-thirty when she saw him near the village entrance at the other end of the marketplace, lined with low trees planted along a path that snaked among the houses. "Alexandre!" she called, but he didn't hear. With remarkable quickness, Blanche ducked under the table, reappearing in the aisle crowded with families goggling at every vegetable and piece of fruit. Jostling three old ladies as she dodged between bodies made slow-witted by the heat, thrusting a hand in the air so that Alexandre, who had his back to the square and was about to cross the street, would see her. When she'd passed the last vendor's stand and the terrace of Le Marché, where Aurore saw her narrowly avoid overturning a table, she flung herself across the lawn, as breathless as if it were a holiday, and scrambled across the street after Alexandre. He was ambling down the sidewalk, hands in his pockets, heading toward the part of the village where his parents lived.

He turned just before she grasped his shoulder. At the sight of Blanche, red-faced and sweating, her hair disheveled, steadying herself with one hand on the wall, a wide smile lit up his handsome face.

"What on earth's gotten into you?" he asked.

"I saw you from the market . . . I called to you, but . . . you didn't hear me so I . . . "

She gasped, sucking in a lungful of air.

"Relax, Blanche."

She straightened abruptly.

"How do you expect me to relax? I haven't heard from you!"

Anger distorted her fine features. Alexandre tried to take her hand, but she jerked it away.

"I thought you'd left again! What game are you playing, Alexandre? Why did you come to the hospital every day? Why are you doing this to me?"

She was screaming. From the other side of the square, on the terrace of Le Marché, Aurore stared at them, her serving tray clutched in one hand. Alexandre took Blanche by the shoulders.

"I thought you all just needed a little time."

Blanche closed her eyes, impervious to the reassuring words. He was gripping her shoulders hard. She let him do it, trembling, accepting it all. Eager, even, for him to touch her.

"Louis wouldn't have let me in. You know that."

He let go of her, dropping his gaze, his face suddenly like a little boy's. Blanche's anger evaporated at the sight of his innocent expression.

"Louis calls all the shots at Paradise."

"I'm sorry," she whispered. "I shouldn't have shouted."

She moved closer. He cupped a hand over his eyes to block out the sun, but Blanche was quicker, putting herself between him and the light, silently offering her lips, hard and impatient on his.

A bell from the past chimed inside her.

For a few seconds, her ears were filled with the warped, distant sound. She could hear it, this furiously chiming bell, the sound swelling and throbbing with each beat of her heart. It was inside her, this strange childhood voice, this eerie instrument, this sharp repeated tone, harder and harder to bear the longer it went on, vibrating from her skull down to her toes.

The bell chimed one last time and she let it take over entirely, so that it would exhaust itself. As the sound faded, the noises of the outside world returned; she couldn't have said who was talking, who was shouting, which child was running between the parked cars in the square, and it took a few seconds more for these familiar sounds to fill her, along with the rasp of Alexandre's breath against her neck, right there in front of everyone.

"Come to Paradise tomorrow," she whispered.

Alexandre didn't reply. His mouth was pressed to her shoulder, his hands on her back, hardly daring to hold her against him; he caressed her very gently, afraid she would crumble at his touch. Blanche could feel a vein pulsing in his neck. Suddenly he didn't seem so sure of himself anymore; his calm had deserted him.

For three weeks, she had thought of nothing but this. She'd fallen asleep remembering that first kiss, in high school, and that first time, in the upstairs bedroom, the pig being slaughtered outside, fallen asleep remembering all the times that had followed. She'd realized that fighting the memories only made them more vivid, every detail strikingly clear. Alexandre was so beautiful, so gentle, his face, even with the damage inflicted by Louis, as perfectly smooth as warm wax, emotions flitting across it lightly, like a fine rain. How she loved that face, those perennial dimples.

When Alexandre had come to the market that first day, when he'd seen her, she had read the joy in his eyes, and her own contempt and the rage and teenage anger still pent up in her woman's body had been powerless against it; in those eyes she had read his affection for her. He hadn't asked for forgiveness, or given excuses; he was just here, back from the city, where he had conquered so many hearts in the intervening years. That doctor, for example, Doctor Neyrie, who had spoken to him like a son; even in the midst of her concern for Émilienne, Blanche had been reassured by the confidence this man, so used to death and injury, to rapid and efficient speech, had shown in Alexandre. He was different; he deserved to be given everything: time, and words, and love. Her love, which she had guarded like a rare delicacy, perishable and fragile.

"Will you come to Paradise tomorrow?" she repeated.

He nodded.

She crossed the street, feeling Alexandre's eyes on her back.

She left the market at three o'clock. Normally, she stopped by the café to see Aurore, but today she drove straight back to Paradise, her mind filled with nothing but him, his taste, the softness of his lips, his flushed face when she'd reproached him for his absence over the past three weeks. Alexandre had come back and Louis had punched him, given him the thrashing of his life. Even now, her fists clenched on the steering wheel, Blanche thought he had deserved that beating, more than anyone. Louis had launched himself at Alexandre and he'd been right to do it. He had to pay for the heartache, the pain his leaving had caused, for the abyss toward which he'd pushed

Blanche, who had spent so many years clinging to the edge, try-ing to pull herself up. Louis had hit him, and then her grand-mother had fallen ill, but Alexandre had saved her. Yes, that was what she believed: Alexandre had saved her grandmother's life. What would have happened if they had waited in that bed-room for a doctor to come at some unspecified time? And that doctor, Doctor Neyrie; would he have seen to Émilienne so quickly if Alexandre hadn't stepped in?

Blanche thought back to those mornings in the lobby, when he'd waited for her amid the tears and the sorrow and the imminent deaths and the bad news. He'd waited for her with perfect composure, as if none of that could ever touch Émilienne or her family, utterly confident in his actions, his decisions. And Blanche had loved him for it. Once again, she'd let herself be seduced by those deep eyes, that sweet smile, those comforting phrases. Alexandre's words didn't pierce her heart with pain anymore; now they soothed her, promised that everything would fall into place; they would take good care of Émilienne, and it would all be fine. He'd said that each morn-ing before leaving for work, and Blanche had believed him, had clung to those words during the three weeks since her grandmother's collapse.

Alexandre hadn't come around in those three weeks. That had been enough time for her to give herself over entirely to the idea that he would never abandon them again, her and Paradise. Going away a second time would have made him a monster, and that was a word Blanche reserved for the calves born with five legs, for one-eyed cats, for all the world's atroc-ities that hovered at the edges of their domain without ever penetrating it.

Blanche loved him.

As she was parking the car in the barn next to the tractor, a wave of dizziness came over her. She breathed deeply for a few seconds, her hands still clutching the wheel, unmoving, her body stiff in the seat that smelled of sweat. She loved him.

"Everything will fall into place."

Blanche heard Louis's footsteps in the yard, a bit heavy, but quick. She wiped her eyes and slapped her cheeks lightly to bring back the color that the dizzy spell had drained from them, and when she pushed open the car door, he extended a hand to help her out, but she brushed the gesture aside.

É milienne would never again be what she had been.
She was still standing, certainly; she hadn't lost her strength of will, but she came downstairs later in the mornings. In the evening, Blanche could hear the stairs creaking and her grandmother breathing hard as she made her way up them; the distance between the front hall and the second floor had become almost insurmountable for her. She never complained in front of Blanche and Louis, but the more time that passed, the more indications her granddaughter saw that she had aged greatly. Émilienne ate less and more slowly. She just wasn't hungry. She laughed less often; when Louis recounted his day the corners of her mouth would twitch, trying to stretch into a proper smile, but very soon her lips would droop again. Blanche wanted desperately to prop the corners of that mouth up with her own fingers, to bring back Émilienne's youth—all those moments when she and Gabriel had shrieked with laughter in the bathtub in front of the house and she'd gazed at them as if seeing them for the first time. Nothing could have wiped the joy from her face at that blissful sight, the certainty that everything was in its right place, and that rightness, sometimes, was as simple as two toddlers in a washtub with a dog romping around them.

As time ravaged Émilienne's body and her memory, those moments of intense happiness left her one by one, becoming foreign to her existence. Soon she began keeping mostly to her chair; each movement, each step, each word undertaken only when absolutely necessary. Little by little, life became limited to the dining room table and her armchair by the window.

Blanche and Louis resigned themselves to the fact that, despite their efforts, she was slipping away from them.

One evening, after the market, Émilienne seemed more exhausted than ever. A churchlike silence reigned over the dinner table; the grandmother ate nothing, scraping at her plate with her knife like a naughty child. Louis watched her hopelessly.

"Alexandre's going to come here," Blanche announced.

Émilienne turned her head very slowly toward Blanche. Louis stopped staring at the old lady's plate.

"Out of the question," he grunted, pushing his own plate away.

"I didn't ask for your opinion."

He pushed back his chair and stood up, as long and thin as a rifle. Émilienne, concentrating on Blanche, didn't seem to notice that he'd moved. Louis went to the door and opened it but, instead of going out, he slammed it, abruptly, violently.

"Stop, Louis," Émilienne whispered. "Stop, all right?"

The sound of her voice had an instant calming effect on him.

"Sorry," he mumbled.

Blanche thought he would sit back down but he planted himself by the window, arms crossed.

"So—he's coming here," Émilienne repeated.

"Yes. I think so."

The old lady set her knife delicately next to her plate.

"That's good."

Blanche heard Louis let out a breath heavy as a stone.

"How can you let him come back here? After what he did to you!"

Blanche buried her face in her hands. Louis paced back and forth near the table, a prisoner of his own anger, of the two women in league against him. He hated Alexandre more than his own father. He hated the man more than anything in the world.

"You can't do this, Blanche," he implored.

This time, she half-turned toward him in her chair.

"You can sleep at Gabriel's, if it's so unbearable for you to see him."

"You don't understand." The words came out in broken shards.

He went to Émilienne and kissed her quickly on the forehead. Very calm all of a sudden, he put a hand on the doorknob. The door opened with a loud creak. Before disappearing into the vestibule, he said, his voice low:

"I won't be able to handle it if he hurts you again."

Like a mechanical doll, Blanche cleared the table and helped her grandmother stand up. Out in the front hall, at the foot of the staircase, she faced Émilienne, took both of her hands, and they went up the stairs together like that.

She guided her without saying anything, without hurrying her, and as she was leaving the bedroom, she heard Émilienne breathing hoarsely behind her, plunged immediately into dreams.

BEING HAPPY

Alexandre came the next day.

Up in her room, Blanche didn't hear the young man knock. At two o'clock in the afternoon, the house, sweltering in the heat, was humming with the sounds of turtle-doves and mice. Sitting on the clean sheets of her bed, knees drawn up, Blanche was gazing out the window at the tree, the color of its curling leaves. Louis hadn't eaten lunch at the farm. His plate was still on the table, "just in case," Émilienne had said, but Blanche knew she wouldn't see him again outside working hours. They'd cross paths in the Bas-Champs, or on the road maybe, or at Gabriel's, but as long as he knew Alexandre had license to enter Paradise, he wouldn't eat at its table. Blanche and Alexandre would have the house to themselves and, above all, Émilienne's approval.

Rocking gently back and forth on the bed, Blanche felt as if she'd reached the end of a long dirt road studded with booby traps. It was a road she'd traveled from childhood to reach this summer afternoon; she had been hurt, had fallen more than once, but now that she was here, at this window, waiting for Alexandre, Blanche believed this was the culmination of an odyssey that was ending here, now, in the clarity of deep emotion. She had achieved what she had never dared to hope for: she was happy. Everything was falling back into place. Émilienne, Alexandre, Paradise.

Alexandre's coming would change everything. She thought anxiously about the dust on the banister, the smell of dampness, the whiteness of the sheets. He was coming to hold her, kiss her. The whole life she wished for waited, now, along with her.

She went down the stairs. A slight breeze wafted in through the half-open door; sunlight fell in a shimmering arrow on the floor and shattered against the wall. Surprised, Blanche took a few steps and froze in the dining room doorway. Alexandre was there, sitting next to Émilienne. Blanche couldn't make out what he was saying, but her grandmother was nodding, repeating, "Good, good." She glanced at Alexandre quickly, then again. The young man had seated himself a modest distance away from the old lady, though still close enough to help her if she wanted to stand. The newspaper was always on the table now; even at dinner, it was merely shoved into a corner, but the rest of the day it was spread out over the whole surface, unfolded. Alexandre was pointing out something on the second-to-last page, while Émilienne continued to murmur "Good, good." They looked as if they might have been the only two people in the world, and Blanche was afraid to disturb this moment of companionship between them, so sudden and so strange for two people who had wrenched themselves apart so violently years ago, in this very room.

"I don't want to interrupt . . . "

Alexandre leapt to his feet.

"We were having a reunion!" he joked. "Émilienne seems much better, I think."

But Blanche didn't want to talk about that, about her grandmother's health or the hours of her exile from Paradise—or the three weeks, more painful still, that had followed without him.

Alexandre had dinner at Paradise that evening. He promised to come back the next day, and in the days after that. Blanche suggested that he stay the night, but it was "impossible."

"Why 'impossible?'" she asked, her green eyes darkening like storm clouds.

Very calmly, Alexandre explained that he had things to do at the office; that he would be moving to the village soon, but first he had to give notice that he was vacating his little apartment in the city, and to figure out the costs of transporting everything. He was thinking of suggesting to his boss that they open a branch of the company out here in the country, to manage farmland business and the needs of new buyers directly without wasting time in the car. And he was in discussions to buy the land behind his parents' place; he wanted to own the meadow, to build a terrace in it, to knock down a wall and add an expansion so that light could enter the narrow little house at last. All of this, he said, meant that he needed to "take care of some things." Blanche took careful note of every word, every name; she asked his address, and the address of his office, and whether his boss was a good person, and for him to tell her about New Zealand. Gabriel had already told her everything, but she wanted to hear the whole story again, and Alexandre, his smile touched with a hint of exasperation, kissed her gently on the forehead and murmured:

"We've got all the time in the world to talk about our lives from before."

She flushed. Her expression was apologetic—sorry for being so hungry for him, sorry for pecking away at him with questions; it was just that she wanted to know everything. Everything.

The days that followed were like a dream, passionate, exquisite.

Alexandre generally arrived at around one o'clock in the afternoon. He had coffee with Émilienne, sometimes bringing marzipan sweets. Blanche watched her grandmother gobble them up, cheeks bulging with the indulgent treats, a hint of childhood blooming again on the aged surface. Alexandre usually spent around an hour with her, talking about the lovely weather or the car in the barn or the health of the cows, or sometimes they didn't speak at all, Émilienne reading the newspaper, Alexandre sipping his coffee and gazing out the window at the ballet of the geese beneath the oak tree. After a few days, he dragged the table out into the yard, beneath the shade of the leafy canopy. He always came just as Louis was passing by; the farmhand never looked up, his face and arms gleaming with sweat; he was just passing, with the chickens and the guinea hens and the ducks, just passing. The only sound he made was the swishing of his coveralls around his legs. Louis was living at Gabriel's. Blanche wondered how they managed, the three of them in that tiny cube on the edge of the woods, but the questions were quickly wiped from her mind by Alexandre's smile.

And so, she gave everything up; she was his, theirs; the time for worrying about others was past. These moments together were all that counted; these hours outside, or in the kitchen, these pieces of the day filled her with joy, with pride, with certainty. She hadn't felt this way for so long that experiencing these emotions now, so strongly, in her flesh and her soul, gave her absolute confidence in the future.

Blanche led him to their room, the way you guide a mule up a hillside. His body against hers, his mouth, the new muscles, the hair that now grew where, years earlier, his skin had been perfectly smooth, and the things he did, too, things he'd done with others first, his kisses, deep, sometimes rough, hungry; his sex. She played with his lips, his thighs, all of him, from his toenails to his hair; all of it enchanted her, all of it was hers to delight in, to nibble, to lick. She devoured him as if she were a starving animal, desire erasing fatigue and anxiety. She was theirs, the past receding; she was theirs, and she murmured it to him over and over as they made love, making up for all the afternoons they had missed; she said it again and again, and Alexandre closed his eyes. They made love noisily, wrapped tightly around each other. When he left to take care of some business, Blanche dozed, limp and contented, her body still pulsing, while beneath the window, out in the yard, Louis worked himself to the breaking point, saturated in the scents of manure and mud and smoke, destroying himself so he wouldn't be destroyed by Alexandre and Blanche, continuing to take care of Paradise like a sad and weary bird still adding twigs to the nest.

T he first night.
Alexandre had said:
"I have a few free days coming up. I could stay, if you want."

Blanche's fingers trailed along his stomach, circling his belly button, traveling up the narrow alley between his pectoral muscles and running along his neck, covering him with caresses, capturing this body that she loved. Alexandre was hers, really hers, alive and well, his heart beating in her ear.

"I want you to stay."

Blanche melted into his arms. The smells of sweat and sex and their breaths rose and mingled.

"Okay. I'll pack some things tomorrow and stay until Monday."

Three nights. Blanche shivered. Tomorrow, Friday, maybe they'd have dinner in the garden; she'd wear her white dress with the red flowers. Émilienne would enjoy a little change. She glanced at the alarm clock on the nightstand. Three in the afternoon.

"You're leaving right now?"

Alexandre was already slowly getting dressed, with almost ridiculous care. His clothes were neatly folded on a chair. Sitting on the edge of the bed, he buttoned his sleeves carefully.

"Alexandre?"

She reached out to him.

"If I'm going to leave the office early tomorrow to get here in time for dinner, I'll have to work later today."

Naked beneath the sheets, Blanche gazed at him admiringly. His back was very straight, his well-cut shirt falling gracefully over his narrow but well-built hips. His shoulders and pectoral muscles, grooved in all the right places, seemed wirier, stronger than they had when he was a teenager. And above that self-assured male body, that face, still astonishingly youthful.

"Until tomorrow, then."

He kissed her forehead, her nose, her mouth. Blanche couldn't move, immobilized by pleasure in this bed filled with the scent of their lovemaking.

The next day seemed to drag on endlessly. Incapable of sleeping late, Blanche was up at six A.M. She came downstairs as soon as she heard Louis slam the door. He still took his morning coffee in the kitchen, very early, while everyone was still asleep. As she listened to him moving cups and chairs and sitting down and getting up, she visualized him accepting Alexandre one day, the two of them talking, perhaps, even asking each other's forgiveness. She persisted in believing that things would fall into place eventually; if Louis didn't want to live under this roof anymore, maybe she could fix up the outbuilding next to the barn for him, so that he could be here without being here, be nearby while still keeping his distance, keep living in Paradise without having to cross that road, twice a day, where Étienne and Marianne had perished. She wondered if he ever thought about that when he saw Gabriel in the evenings, or when he was crossing that thin strip of asphalt to the house, but then she remembered that he'd never had anything to do with them; Louis didn't share his traits or his blood with this family; he wasn't her brother, or her cousin, or her uncle, just a man who had washed up in Paradise.

Once he had left the kitchen, she went downstairs, made a pot of coffee and a plentiful breakfast. She spent the morning cleaning the house, changing the sheets, polishing the stairs, sweeping the yard all the way to the dirt road. Beneath the tree, she set out wedges for the table, comfortable chairs, and a sky-blue tablecloth. They'd have a late dinner, after it had cooled down outside. In the afternoon, she went into the village and bought pretty paper napkins and a bottle of red wine. Aurore waved to her from a distance. She got back to Paradise at about five o'clock, where Émilienne was waiting for her in the kitchen. Her grandmother suggested that she style her hair the way Marianne used to do, in a low bun with loose wisps curling around her face. The dress lay clean and ironed on her bed. Blanche took a bath. For an instant, the memory of her grandmother gently scrubbing her shoulders flashed through her memory; then she washed herself with slow strokes, inspecting her own body. The mirror was too small to see all of herself at once; part of her was missing, but it didn't matter. She gazed at herself, pinching her buttocks to make them rosy, running her index finger along the curve from breast to thigh. Blanche had never felt so beautiful as she did in this moment, in front of this broken mirror.

Alexandre arrived late in the afternoon, an overnight bag in one hand and a net bag of delicacies in the other. He'd brought fruit, a meringue pie for dessert, bonbons, mint chocolate, marzipan, tea. He put it all in the kitchen and then cleared a shelf in the refrigerator for the pie, which, he said, should be kept in a cool place, covered with paper towels. Meticulously, he cut the chocolate into little squares, which he arranged on a plate, a semicircle of orange wedges in the center, mint on either side, and two marzipan drops for eyes in this sugared face on the chipped plate. Closing the door behind him he murmured, "This will be pretty for dessert," and Blanche kissed him on the lips. She loved it when he talked like that; coming from his mouth everything was charming, adorable; he was so sweet with his timeless way of being, old-fashioned and modern at once, so certain that nothing, no one, could resist him.

They ate dinner outside. The evening stretched like a cat on a cushion. Émilienne asked after Alexandre's parents; they were getting older, but they were fine; his father would work one more year at the ticket window in the train station, with Aurore's father, before retiring. Alexandre was planning to buy the land behind the house so their golden years would be comfortable ones, filled with light, the horizon no longer blocked by pale, ugly walls. Blanche watched him; he was focused on Émilienne, looking her straight in the eye, as if her opinion were more important than anything. For these long moments before dessert, Blanche accepted that, for the two of them, she didn't exist. She needed for Alexandre to love her grandmother, needed to be certain that he did, that he would take care of her, that he would be here. She coughed softly, to draw his attention from their conversation. He flashed her one of those smiles that she adored and began to clear the table as deftly as if he were a seasoned waiter. As he disappeared into the house, his arms loaded with dirty plates and empty dishes and glasses, Émilienne leaned toward Blanche.

"He's serious. I can tell he's serious."

He returned a few minutes later, an apron tied loosely around his waist, with the pie on a serving platter and his plate with the face made of chocolates and marzipan.

"And now, a selection of desserts."

Émilienne applauded. Blanche, from the depths of her chair, wished this moment would never end. They were beautiful, the three of them, on this still evening, in front of this everlasting house; they were beautiful, after all they'd been through, relaxing in the cool air, sated with food and wine and tenderness.

They didn't go back inside until it was very late. Blanche washed the dishes while Alexandre helped Émilienne upstairs.

The steps creaked beneath their weight. From the kitchen, she traced their path, their movements. She lifted the plates out of the basin of dirty water and lined them up to dry next to the sink. As silence fell upstairs, she felt a new emotion welling: the sense that everything was all right; everything was as it should be. Just as he'd promised.

The night, clear and silent, enveloped the house. Blanche watched the dance of the nocturnal butterflies, drawn by the lightbulb above the sink. She reached for the switch, but a hand closed on her arm, eliciting a cry of surprise.

He had stolen up noiselessly behind her. Blanche, caught between Alexandre's body and the edge of the sink, tried to turn around but he prevented her.

He was already teasing her; in trying to disengage herself Blanche could feel his hands, his torso, his sex. A long sigh rose in her throat. Alexandre, his hands at her middle, solidly gripping her waist, could feel her excitement: she was his, theirs, and here, as the plates dried in the night on a damp cloth, Blanche surrendered to the weight of Alexandre's body, and of the long wait.

FALLING

The window cast an eye over the yard. The long shadows of the tree's branches extended all the way to the barn; the dog stretched its paws, protecting itself from the heat by shifting position to follow the dance of sun through the leaves. At noon, Émilienne found it stretched out on the steps in the shade. She didn't scold it; she might even have stroked it, which happened sometimes, running a hand along its back and patting it on the top of the head between the ears. The animal blinked with pleasure and went back to sleep.

Blanche had woken at sunrise. Alexandre was asleep next to her, his face turned toward her, his breathing slow, almost inaudible. She drank in the sight of his long body given over to dreams; in the early morning light it looked like the dog's on the porch steps. Alexandre was sleeping heavily, despite not having drunk much last night. At nine o'clock he turned over. Blanche thought he was going to reach for his watch on the nightstand but no, he went back to sleep in a rustle of sheets. Blanche had never stayed in bed so late, with or without Alexandre, and she had the exquisite sense of breaking the house rules. Stay in bed; why not? Louis was taking care of everything outside; it was what he was paid for. She had every right to stay in this room for hours, whole days even, with this male body, this canine body, next to her, hard and straight as the edge of a watering trough.

"ALEXANDRE!"

She jumped. For a split second she thought she'd fallen back to sleep, that the cry had happened in a dream. Still groggy, she listened. Next to her, Alexandre slept on.

"ALEXANDRE!"

This time, she hadn't dreamed it.

"What's going on?" he mumbled. "What time is it?"

He seized his watch. Nine-thirty. He rubbed his eyes. The gesture, mechanical and precise, smoothed away the traces of the night as if by magic.

"Someone's calling you."

Louis's voice. Blanche wanted to go down, to tell him to cut out whatever game he was playing at, that this wasn't the time, not here, not now, not in this house. But that second time, there had been something in his voice, a tone she didn't recognize, ominous. The shout hadn't been aggressive. Loaded with meaning, maybe, but not aggressive.

"Yes, yes, I heard you."

Alexandre unfolded himself to perch on the edge of the bed. His clothes, on the chair, were as immaculate as if a valet had laid them out.

"Alexandre! Come down here!"

Blanche leapt out of bed and slipped on the robe she kept hanging from a hook on the wall. It was too warm, and she felt as if she were smothering. Alexandre dressed quickly. The serenity of sleep had left his face; all Blanche saw now was the frown, the mulish expression. He didn't bother to button his sleeves or lace his dress shoes. Before going downstairs, he looked back at her and managed a thin smile.

From the top of the stairs, she could see that he had stopped short in the front hall. Louis, in the doorway of the dining room, was staring outside. No one spoke. Blanche felt the breeze rising up the stairs, already hot. Something, someone was there. A deathly silence hung in the air.

"Is everything all right?"

Émilienne, calling from the kitchen. Louis turned.

"Stay where you are; everything's fine."

Émilienne appeared, alarmed by the bad tidings she sensed in his voice, and she, too, froze in the hall.

The first few steps at the top of the staircase creaked under Blanche's weight. Alexandre, Louis, and Émilienne turned in a single movement, all three of their bodies tensing, begging her to stay put, to go back to her room.

"Why are you looking at me like that?" she asked, her throat suddenly tight, her feet bare on the wood she'd polished yesterday.

Alexandre hung his head. He gave a long sigh. Blanche, hearing it, hurried down the stairs, one hand on the banister, the other clutching the knotted belt of her robe.

When she reached the bottom, Louis put his body between her and Alexandre.

"Blanche, you shouldn't stay here."

But she shoved him aside, violently, and before Louis could restrain her, she stepped out into the daylight, coming to a sudden halt on the porch.

A young woman stood there, waiting. She wore a blue dress with elbow-length sleeves and intricately woven sandals. Blanche stared at her. She was slim, with a face like a cover model; slightly too thin, perhaps, but delicately built.

Clutching her hand, a child.

Curly hair. Almond-shaped eyes. Dimples. An adorable face. Cheeks made rosy by the sun. He stared at Blanche with a look she recognized.

"I'm sorry," the young woman said, in a voice so soft that Blanche had to strain to hear it, "is Alexandre here?"

She glanced at Louis, who nodded.

"His office told me he was working here today."

Blanche sensed Alexandre backing toward the staircase.

"They . . . they told you he was *working* here?" she stammered.

The other woman seemed so sweet, so submissive. Blanche didn't doubt her word. This woman, the kind mothers marry to their sons without a qualm, the kind you welcome unconcernedly into the family. This woman was telling the truth, and her words crushed Blanche. Her gaze fixed on the child, unable to move, Blanche stretched an arm behind her, pointing at Alexandre without looking at him, and whispered:

"Get out."

The little boy began to cry, miserable in the stifling heat. His mother picked him, murmuring, "Now, now, we're almost finished here." Émilienne vanished into the dining room. The young woman, embarrassed, spoke to Alexandre:

"The little one wanted to see you; you haven't been home much this week, and I thought it would be a nice surprise for us to come out to your village."

Alexandre groaned.

"This isn't a good time," he managed finally, in a strangled voice.

The young woman shook her head. The little boy laid his own head on her shoulder.

"You even work on Saturdays, I see."

Blanche let out a growl. Louis, Alexandre, and the unknown woman all jumped at the same time. The child hiccupped violently. Blanche wanted to cry, too. But Marianne was dead, and Émilienne was old. There was no one to protect her.

"Come on, Blanche."

Louis had stepped in front of Alexandre. He stood above Blanche on the doorstep and took her arm, firmly. She let him do it. He drew her back inside. She looked at Alexandre.

"Tell me it isn't true," she said. Begged.

Head down, unmoving, Alexandre sniffed.

"I'm sorry, Blanche, truly sorry."

She wanted to launch herself at him, but Louis pushed her back, stepping between her and her love. She tried to free herself, but he gripped her arms.

"I just want a good life," Alexandre whispered.

The couple left together. The wife hesitated for a few seconds, as if to turn back toward Blanche, but her husband took hold of her shoulder where it met her neck, leading her where he wanted to go, far from here, far from Paradise. Through the window, the young woman and the young man, the boy between them, walking together in a neat little row, made a perfect tableau. The soft light of morning fell gently on them. Their feet crunched on the gravel edging the yard and, as they walked away, Blanche, white and stunned, made her way slowly into the kitchen, Louis supporting her.

It was as if her muscles had turned to cotton. In the little passage flooded with light, Blanche, held up by the farmhand, cast her shadow on the floor. Her face seemed to be spilling down over her throat, her chest. Her body remained upright through pure reflex, but inside, her whole soul, the soul made up of all the ages she had been, all the experiences she had had, caved in.

É milienne wept.

Fat tears streamed down her cheeks. Blanche and Louis sat in their usual places, the old lady presiding over the miserable gathering, arms crossed on the closed news-paper, slumped shoulders unmoving. The tears fell from her cheeks and dripped on her fingers. Blanche had never seen her cry. She felt almost embarrassed, but her own heart, heavy and swollen, made it impossible to have any real thoughts. Focusing on anything other than the young wife and her little son standing there in front of the house was beyond her capac-ity. Across from her, Louis, reeling under the impact of their heartbreak, tried to conceal his fury by rubbing his hands together. His palms were bright red. Blanche thought they might start to bleed. It didn't take away the pain that out-weighed everything else, but it was helping him put his thoughts in order.

"It's my fault."

Émilienne's voice was unrecognizable, choked with tears, and guilt, and age.

"It's my fault, Blanche."

Blanche covered her grandmother's hand with her own. Émilienne let her do it. Drowning in grief, she sat there word-lessly.

"Tell us what you mean," Blanche prompted her, gently.

So, she told them everything. Blanche leaned forward intently, trying to grasp every word. Louis listened, unmoving, frozen.

At the hospital, every morning, Alexandre had come to see Émilienne. On the first day, he had merely sat in the chair next to her bed without speaking. The grandmother, her senses dulled by drugs and exhaustion, hadn't pressed him. She enjoyed his presence; he watched over her until Blanche arrived, and when he left, he always said:

"Don't worry, Émilienne. Blanche is coming."

They hadn't been just quick visits like the others thought. He'd stayed for an hour, sometimes longer. Émilienne had been sure her granddaughter knew about it, that she approved. Blanche shuddered.

On the second day, Alexandre had apologized to Émilienne.

"I'm so sorry. I know I hurt all of you."

He wanted to make things right. He was coming back to live in the village; he'd already left the city behind, a distant memory. Alexandre had "thought about things long and hard, from every angle." And Émilienne, in her bed, in her suffering, listened to this boy describe his feelings to her. He loved Blanche, more than anything. If taking care of Paradise was what it would take for the grandmother to forgive him, to trust him, he would do it.

In the days that followed, he assured her that he had thought of everything, planned everything so that Paradise's future, and Blanche's, would be guaranteed. He explained to Émilienne, in her sickness and exhaustion, that it would be necessary to sell off some of the land, the least productive parts, in order to provide themselves with the means to make better use of the rest. They would need to replace some of the farm equipment, and to farm a smaller area. It was too difficult, this life, as Émilienne knew, of course; too hard. It was no life for a modern young woman. They would have to relieve some of this weight, this burden on her, so that she could be happy, and think about things other than work.

Louis let out a curse. Blanche was utterly still. She listened to the story and she watched the trap closing on Émilienne and she understood, a dreadful hint of pity stealing into her eyes, that her grandmother had allowed herself to be hoodwinked.

"I'm not going to live much longer . . . " the old woman murmured. "He made a good case . . . "

"Six thousand per hectare," said Louis.

The two women stared at him.

"What?"

"Six thousand per hectare. That's the price around here."

Blanche's face sagged.

All of that, just to build, and sell, and build again, and sell again. Alexandre had fucked her. For the first time, she felt like there was no other word for it: he had fucked her, and she had let him. Had even asked for it.

"What happened then?" she asked Émilienne.

"After that he disappeared for three weeks, as you know," said her grandmother, straightening slightly in her chair.

She had drained herself completely of tears.

"I couldn't talk to you about it. You would have said no."

Émilienne was right; Blanche would have refused even to discuss it. That was why Alexandre had stayed away for three weeks: to give the old lady time to worry about the future, to fear death, and the paucity of the inheritance she was leaving behind, and the burden maintaining this land represented.

"When the two of you got back together, it was perfect. I'd dreamed of it."

Blanche thought back to the days when Alexandre and Émilienne had drunk coffee together, whispering, their heads bent close. Alexandre had come back; he would take care of everything. The sale of the hectares of land around the pond would pay for new milking machines and the cost of extending the barn, and for more animals to enlarge the herd. It was modernizing, allowing themselves a little less harshness, a little more comfort.

"Everything seemed to be falling into place," Émilienne whispered.

Louis was silent. Blanche was afraid to look at him. They'd forgotten him. They'd even driven him out of Paradise, which was what Alexandre had wanted from the beginning. A skilled strategist, Alexandre had stayed away, pretending to be afraid of Louis; at every turn he'd portrayed himself as a victim of the farmhand, and Blanche realized it only now, in defeat. She saw the stages of his plan unfurling before her eyes now, one by one. The memory of every one of his smiles scalded her now; he had been laughing at her, at Louis, at Émilienne. He'd been laughing at her love. And, even worse, he'd made her eat dirt.

"Yesterday, when he showed up with his overnight bag and his gifts, everything seemed so lovely," Émilienne murmured.

"Have you signed anything?" demanded Louis, abruptly.

"Yes."

He stood up, flinging his chair back against the wall, and stalked out of the dining room. Out in the front hall, he let out a long cry, like the scream of a horse, guttural, terrible. Émilienne pulled her hand from beneath Blanche's and pressed her palms to her ears; in Louis's howling she could hear all his innocence, his naivete, his fear of dying.

The old woman wiped her eyes, rubbing them so hard that it seemed as if her fingers were actually digging into the sockets, the movement slow and uncharacteristic.

"Why did you do that?"

Blanche could hear a *something* in her own voice, like a broken bell, quivering between her teeth and beneath her tongue and roiling in her throat, a cold manifestation of horror that was growing heavier and heavier, taking up the space between her words, between her thoughts, between the tears that were to come. Yes, the tears would come. But not in front of the others.

"Because I wanted to do things right before going."

Blanche almost said, "Going where?" Her grandmother

was old, very old, and Blanche knew nothing about that, about the questions people ask themselves before dying, or their last wishes, or the agony of not knowing whether this night will be the last, or if there will be one more, or ten, or a hundred. But Blanche had known death earlier than the others, and now that Émilienne was approaching her own end, on the slippery edge of a cliff, Blanche was watching her disappear, little by little, beyond the horizon of Paradise.

"What does he want to do with the land?"

"Sell it."

Blanche pictured what Paradise might look like in ten years, honeycombed with lots and second homes and campsites all around Sombre-Étang and in the Bas-Champs.

"I don't understand," she whispered. "It's not legal to build around here."

"Not yet."

Blanche frowned. She'd always been told, both in school and at home, that this was protected land.

"What do you mean?"

Émilienne sighed. "Don't you see what's happening out there?"

"No. I don't."

Houses would soon be built; identical, practical houses, like endless sets of twins. The city would arrive with its grasping arms of asphalt and paint and tolls, it would come all the way to Paradise, and Paradise would become part of the spreading city. Men and animals would die so that cities could continue to grow, all-consuming.

Blanche swayed in her chair. The dam broke behind the green of her eyes, so beautiful, the green of water and drenched leaves. In ten years, or perhaps even less, the world would begin to nibble away at their land. And Alexandre had taken the first bite.

Here they were, then, the tears, real ones. Bouts of weeping overtook her at all hours of the day and night, rising from the depths of her heart, drowning everything in their path, crushing this body that work in the fields had made strong and solid, methodically destroying the ability to think clearly. They irrigated her face, leaving behind salty riverbeds in which Blanche's memories lay like dogs starved to stop them from barking. Here they were, then, the tears, real ones. Torrents of shame, of incomprehension, words of consolation butting against them. Blanche, bereft of food and fresh air and tenderness, curled and shrank in the big bed that still smelled of Alexandre despite its sheets being changed. Her body withered, cracking, and Blanche refrained from filling it so as not to fuel her tears, not to taste the saltiness any more on her dry lips, seamed with a thin, bright line. Blanche was starving to death in her big bed; behind the door, Émilienne waited. She couldn't bathe her now, or carry her, or soothe her the way she had before. Now Blanche was alone in her pain.

Here they were, then, the tears, real ones. An avalanche of wounds, her muscles and skin and bones and blood trying to escape through her eyes, fleeing this unmoored vessel, this wreck incapable of accommodating any sailors but those of the past, its deck long since collapsed beneath the weight of the bell, enormous now, monstrous, a massive sphere still growing even now. Here they were, then, the tears, the triumph of despair.

They didn't call the doctor. Louis kept on working. In the morning, he ate his breakfast alone in the dining room, flies buzzing in circles above his head, flitting in and out through the open window. Émilienne got up later; he helped her downstairs, made her a coffee and some bread and butter that she hardly touched. Not for anything in the world would he let himself be defeated by the deathly silence. Outside, life was going on; the cows whipped the air with their tails, the chickens scratched and clucked whenever they heard a bird scurrying up the slope, the pigs crowded against the gate of the pen. Louis took care of everything, crossing the yard twenty times a day, looking up at the bedroom, the half-open window sometimes giving him hope that he might glimpse Blanche's face. She was in bed, sinking quietly into her grief, surrendering to the torment of memory, more alive than any of the members of this household where the animals still flocked, moving along despite the absence of the women, huddled in their pain. Louis had moved back into the house; his room felt so large and the house so full of Alexandre's trap. He would have preferred to sleep with the livestock, so afraid was he of being contaminated by misery.

And when he heard Blanche tossing in her bed on the other side of the wall, he thought, *Here they are, then, the tears.*

É milienne set plates in front of the bedroom door. The bread and meat and potatoes disappeared, but she and Louis weren't sure if it was the work of Blanche or a mouse. She came out to go to the bathroom or take a shower, locking the door behind her, just long enough to rinse off with cold water. Anything that eased the pain in her soul, anything that pulled her, even for a few seconds, from the bottomless pit into which Alexandre had shoved her, anything, even the jet of icy water that left red welts on her skin, she accepted it all. But she remained upstairs, wallowing between her sheets or sitting on the edge of the bed by the window. She was disintegrating between those four walls, her skin dreadfully pale, burning pink at the merest touch of sunlight. She went round and round in circles in that strange laboratory made of nothing, both the mad scientist and the guinea pig at once, rummaging in what remained of her carcass, trying to assemble a new person from the leftovers, a strong person, someone who could no longer be hurt, humiliated, destroyed this way.

One morning, at the time when Émilienne usually set down her breakfast plate, Blanche heard three light knocks. She didn't answer.

Three more light knocks.

"Blanche, it's Louis."

She shook her head the way donkeys do when they're trying to shoo away the flies buzzing around their faces.

"Blanche, I have something to tell you."

She crept toward the door, timidly, trying not to make the

floorboards creak, not to make Louis think she was about to open up for him.

"You don't need to open the door. Knock once if you can hear me."

She did it. On the other side of the heavy wooden door, Louis sighed.

"You're going to have to come out eventually, Blanche. You can't stay shut up in there forever."

She took a step backwards, nausea welling up inside her.

"Everything is so beautiful outside," he said, softly, in a voice that was almost tender, a voice Blanche had never heard him use.

She felt heavy. She was so familiar with the old floorboards in her bedroom that she knew exactly where to stop to make it seem like the room was empty.

"Blanche?" Louis murmured.

She reached out a hand and pressed her palm to the door, making the wood creak.

"Gabriel and Aurore are getting married."

Then Louis turned away.

S he didn't touch her plate, not that day, or the next day, or the next.

Her brother was in love with a young woman. Her brother, so ill-suited to life, had found love. Soon, *they* would be married. Blanche sat on the edge of the bed, a grotesque smile pasted on her face, hiccupping. Gabriel had bypassed the farm. He looked at Aurore with eyes overflowing with gratitude and tenderness, protecting her from rural life, from its hardness and efficiency, while she protected him from the endless daydreams in which he'd been lost. Gabriel and Aurore completed each other. They were good together.

Blanche had been happy with Alexandre. Never relaxed or replete, but happy. She was sure of it. For several months, aged seventeen, she had known the power of emotion. At thirty, the return of that emotion to her life had filled her with certainty. How long had they been happy together? A few months, and then, years later, a few weeks.

And now she was paying for that happiness with her whole life, her own tortured body, her jealous memory, and her humiliated soul. She and Alexandre should have gotten married too, lived here, been beautiful the way they had always been beautiful, dimples and green eyes united, on the edge of the pond Émilienne had sold too quickly to save Paradise, to save Blanche.

Gabriel loved, and he was loved. This simple truth devastated his sister; she had been so convinced that he would never be able to cope with life. Knowing him to be so secure, so strong in his relationship forced her to confront her own lies, to accept that Gabriel wasn't going to be just her little brother anymore, but soon the husband of a wife, living proof that he didn't need Blanche, or Émilienne, or Louis. In her older-sibling arrogance, in the sense of responsibility she had borne since childhood, Blanche had forgotten that Paradise wasn't inhabited solely by animals, but also by human beings capable of anything, even of better things.

Sitting down on the wooden floor, Blanche pulled out her father's box, the one full of his notebooks and his writings and photos. She opened "A brief history of Paradise" again. In the middle of the first page, the snapshot of the little Émards.

Blanche and Gabriel, in the washtub. Naked. Bony, for children of that age. Blanche gazed at her wrists in the picture; not eating took her back to those early childhood years, sapped of strength. At thirty years old, Blanche was more fragile than she had been at five, in that iron washtub Émilienne must have had to fill and leave out in the sun to warm the water. The dog, its snout against the handle, lapping with a long, long tongue at the bathwater of these two children splashing around in the heat of a summer's afternoon. Blanche examined the photo for a very long time, searching for some sign to reassure herself, to overcome the loss of Alexandre. But the child she had been didn't look back at her; the little Émard girl beat her hands in the water, her face wet and triumphant, the dog taking advantage of her joy to drink behind her back, and it seemed to Blanche as if her own childhood was mocking her, that right at this exact moment she couldn't rely on it, that the people in the image didn't care about her pain.

Blanche ran a long, dirty fingernail beneath the snapshot, which came away easily from the page. She wanted to slip it beneath her pillow. But on the back of the photo she saw that her father had written a few words in his beautiful cursive, the writing of a disciplined man:

This Sunday, we dragged the big washtub to the edge of the pond. Marianne didn't want the little ones to swim in the muddy water. You can only see the children in the picture; you have to imagine Émilienne dipping her feet in the water, Marianne trying to push the dog away, and me, not talking, because this is where the world stops and happiness starts.

The text, written in beautiful script, took up the whole back of the little square. Blanche squinted to make out each letter, so closely were they squeezed together.

The Émards' daughter read her father's message ten times. She pictured her grandmother, younger, sitting at the edge of the pond; Blanche hadn't even quite been five years old when the photo was taken, but her memory had retained every detail of the place, the moment, the other people in it. The dog hadn't been playing with them, just drinking the bathwater. Marianne had scolded it, undoubtedly hissing, "Get away, get away," to the great amusement of her sun-dazzled husband. Blanche felt her heart—or what was left of it—rotting in her chest like a blackened, empty piece of fruit. The land of happiness, Étienne's promised land, had been sold.

Sold.

Blanche repeated the word, rocking back and forth, sick, crazed, starved, singing a hopeless melody: land. Drained of tears, the orphaned girl bit the inside of her cheeks until blood flowed down her throat. Its taste soothed her instantly; she loved its texture, its thickness, its warmth. For weeks, she had been so cold. The blood revived her mind, her muscles, and her desire. And then Alexandre's betrayal became so clear, so precise, that she almost fainted: for him she had lost her love, her dignity, and her land.

Even beyond her own life, in buying the land that contained the pond, Alexandre was robbing Étienne of the happiness he had found here, wiping out with one signature at the bottom of a contract the life of the Émard family when it was still solid, still rooted. He had given himself the right to draw a line through those children, that washtub, that dog lapping the water from it.

Blanche crawled on all fours along the wooden floor where she had first seen Louis, lying there, his face distorted by his father's blows. Half-conscious, she thought she could see the farmhand's face in the walls, the colors shifting, his eyes now empty, now black and full. The floor scraped her knees and Louis's face disappeared, feature by feature, to be replaced by that of Alexandre. Blanche shook her head to banish the image but, on the wall, the mouth of her great love was forming words she couldn't hear. Daylight filtered through the closed shutters, the rays slashing the throat of Alexandre's memory.

She cowered in a corner of the room. In front of her, the unmade bed, the locked door, the box with its lid pulled aside, the notebook on the floor. Her whole life contained in this dark room, around this bed that had known Marianne and Étienne's lovemaking, and Blanche and Alexandre's. The Émards' daughter saw herself lying against the pillows, in the arms of the man she loved, who didn't love her back.

The memory of their embraces made her stomach clench, cramps doubling her over. Groaning, Blanche lifted her head, both arms wrapped around her middle, and above her head, all along the baseboards and the windows she counted the daddy longlegs and spiders, spinning on their webs. In the half-light it was difficult for Blanche to make them out; two of them moved to within a few centimeters of her head, their webs swaying, and Blanche watched the tiny dancing feet, eyes half-closed, the cramps receding. As soon as she could straighten up without pain, Blanche plucked the spider nearest to her mouth and repeated her act of twelve years earlier, swallowing it without chewing, sensing nothing on her tongue but a faint tang. Her movement had caused a second spider to fall. It lay near her ankle. Very quickly she seized it and sent it, whole, down her throat. Shivers ran through Blanche's body, greedy, avid, like a bird beating its wings between her breasts and her sex, demanding to be fed, famished, imploring, and Blanche, aroused by the taste of blood and chitin, scrutinized every centimeter of the wall in search of another living being to devour.

In the days that followed, she was a beast, eating the animals she could trap within the pathetic confines of her bedroom, her eyes accustomed to the half-light, her body coming apart. She didn't sleep until her work was accomplished, and when she woke, the hunt began again. The morning after that first feast, she opened the window to let in any creatures lurking in the environs; she thought a mouse might scurry through the room, and then she would have no mercy, none.

Little by little, Blanche began to recover. But the days passed, and the plates set in front of the bedroom door returned, full, to the dining room table. Louis worried; he could hear Blanche moving around, he called out to her, she didn't respond, and yet he could hear her distinctly. Sometimes it even seemed like she was jumping, clinging futilely to the walls. Louis wondered where she was getting the energy for it, and Émilienne, watching her assistant's face darken with anxiety, kept repeating:

"What a racket!"

Louis didn't have the strength to laugh. At night he dreamed that he broke down the door of Blanche's room and carried her into his own, settling her in his bed and sleeping at her feet on the floor like a faithful dog, on the alert for the slightest noise of distress, ready to do anything and everything to help her get over Alexandre.

L ouis?"
The farmhand stared at Blanche, stunned.
"You need to eat something," Émilienne chided.
Blanche didn't even look up. "I'm not hungry."

"I don't care," replied her grandmother, pushing a full plate toward her. "You have to eat."

Blanche's ghost occupied the room, step by step. Her body seemed as light as her breathing was heavy, every movement weighing on that chest that rose and fell with such difficulty. The tracery of veins beneath skin stripped of its vibrant color looked like twisted flower stems on her arms, her neck, her temples. She was losing her hair, which floated wispily around her head. Louis watched strands of it drift to the floor and he wanted to scramble for them, to gather them into a bouquet to give to her. They hadn't heard her come downstairs; the floorboards no longer creaked under her weight. The staircase, which usually squeaked so noisily, hadn't made a sound.

The young woman sat down at the table. Her body, horrifyingly thin, seemed as if it might collapse into a heap of bones at any second. Louis avoided looking anywhere but at her big green eyes, so distressing to him was the sight of her fleshless arms and skeletal legs. Blanche had disappeared; nothing remained of her but eyes and pain.

"Louis, I want you to take a vacation," she said.

"Like hell!"

He was wolfing down his potatoes as if he hadn't eaten for months. Blanche read the fatigue in the stiffness of his movements, his hunched shoulders. Louis was forty-one years old but, at this table, at this time of day when the white glare of the sun was merciless, he looked ten years older.

"Louis, you're going to take a vacation. Two weeks, at least. If you don't, I'll fire you," Blanche said, coolly, dispassionately.

He looked up from his plate. His hand, suspended in the air, sketched faint circles, digging an invisible tunnel between them.

"You wouldn't do that."

"Right now, I'm ready to do anything."

Émilienne nodded.

"Do as she says, Louis."

B lanche took over the next morning, starting at five o'clock. First the cows, which she called, and which came, slowly.

"No, I'm not Louis," she said to them, impatiently. "But that's no reason to make me wait."

Next, the chickens. She washed the car, made Émilienne's breakfast, went to Gabriel's house and asked him to handle things at the market for the next few weeks. Dumbfounded at the sight of his sister's body, Gabriel couldn't say a word. Blanche congratulated him on his upcoming wedding. "I'm here if you need anything," she added. Gabriel stared at her uncomfortably, wide-eyed, and murmured a quick *thank you* that stood for all the rest, all they had never said to each other.

In the afternoon, Blanche walked down to the village. Every step felt like a hundred, so weak was she, but she drew energy from the fury that dwelled inside her. At Le Marché, she sat at a table on the terrace and ordered a beer; it had been so long since she'd had one, especially so early in the day. Aurore brought it to her. The terrace was deserted. Aurore offered to make her something to eat, a little plate of something; she was so pale, so thin, that Aurore wondered how she was even able to hold herself upright. "It doesn't matter; I can manage," Blanche snapped. Then she paid, leaving Aurore alone next to the wobbly table in this forgotten village that still bore the traces of Alexandre's passage through it.

On the road to Paradise, she paused at the hairpin curve where her parents had died. There was nothing to indicate that a tragedy had happened here; the grass was as green as the eyes of the Émard women, the trees very tall, a chainsaw rumbling somewhere in the distance. The asphalt cut a wide black smile through the face of the forest. Blanche made her way down to the pigpen, where she stood among the wild grasses, murmuring, "Everything will fall into place."

When she got back to the farm, her body stiff, Blanche went to the little shed where there was an iron faucet above a cement slab perforated with holes where Louis emptied the soured milk and the dirty water from the animals' drinking troughs. The shed, damp in every season, sat in a hollow between the path to the pigpen and the outbuilding where they stored hay and straw. Louis washed his hands here before returning to the house; in the summers, he would stick his head under the faucet and let the icy water cascade down his back, his muscles flexing beneath his taut skin, marked on the knees and elbows and ankles from the constant friction of his work coveralls, and from crowding cows and nuzzling pigs and the dog's tail wagging in the yard. Louis was used to being knocked around. When these slaps and bites and scratches came from Paradise, he kept his head down and accepted the slight pain indulgently, resignedly.

Coming out of the chicken coop on the day before his forced vacation, Louis had watched Blanche bypass the barn and vanish into the hollow. He'd blinked, surprised when she didn't return right away, not having seen her go in the direction of the pigpen, much less the little shed, in weeks. Louis had set down his pail of grain, bringing a dozen guinea hens scuttling around his feet, and, picking his way through feathers and piles of chicken droppings, had crept after her noiselessly. The farm was humming with the last songs of the spring. Soon the summer would lock men and animals in its fiery prison. Swallows sought out the cool air on the edge of Sombre-Étang, and yellow-bellied toads sang their hymns among the boxwoods, the boughs of the tall trees trapping and holding the gentle melodies. Louis could feel a million tiny feet crawling in the hollows of his shoulders, but he didn't dare slap them away for fear that Blanche would notice his presence. When he reached the corner of the barn, in front of the path choked with tall grass and stinging nettles, he pressed himself to the wall, his back very straight, head bent forward.

Blanche was crouching on the concrete slab, her hair loose, legs apart, drinking the cold water thirstily, her neck bent at an odd angle beneath the faucet. Bile rose in Louis's throat: Blanche's arms hung uselessly at her sides, her cheekbones jutting sharply. She drank for a long moment, hardly pausing to breathe, gulping the icy water as if to fill herself up. When she had finished, Louis shrank back, thinking she would turn back to the house, but then he heard the scraping of her trousers against the concrete slab. He leaned forward again.

Blanche was still on her knees. Her trousers were lying on the grass, her matchstick calves, drawn up beneath her thighs, flushing red. Water was still flowing from the faucet. Blanche used the flat of her hand to direct the stream between her thighs, holding on to the faucet with one hand, using the other to guide the jet of water—*so cold*, Louis thought—at her sex, into it, rubbing it so hard that Louis could feel, in the pit of his stomach, the burns the movement and the cold water were inflicting on her. With stiff-jointed, long-nailed fingers she polished the cleft in which Alexandre had buried himself so many times, into which she had agreed and wanted and begged for him to plunge again. Now, beneath Louis's stunned gaze, she was emptying herself of Alexandre, scratching her walls until they bled, washing away the traces of his passage, the remains of their afternoons entangled in the sheets embroidered with the Émard family's initials. She cleaned herself like a wounded animal, shriveled into herself, half-naked, the water flowing over her thighs and soaking into the ground with the milk and the dung and the slime and the little that Alexandre had left behind of himself. She rubbed herself so hard, that blood seeped between her fingers and streamed along the groove in the concrete slab.

Here, in the realm of the chickens, the pail emptied of its grain had been poorly received. The geese had plunged their beaks into it and, finding nothing, screeched in concert. Louis had kicked them away. He was due to leave the next day.

The ten days that followed resembled that first morning. The cows, the chickens, Émilienne, Gabriel, Le Marché, Aurore. The pause at the hairpin curve. Every day she repeated, "If either of you need anything at all, please don't hesitate to ask." She hardly ate. Slept even less. At night, she put Émilienne to bed. Sometimes she smoked a cigarette on the front steps of Paradise. Louis maintained radio silence. She wasn't worried; he would be back. Wherever he was, he would come back. She was sure of it. The rest didn't matter anymore. Only Paradise counted, and the people and animals it sheltered.

Three days before the farmhand was scheduled to return, at nine-thirty in the morning, she called the office where Alexandre worked. A young woman asked her to hold for a moment.

"Hello, this is Alexandre, your advisor. How can I help you?"

"It's Blanche."

Silence on the other end of the line. She could hear the sounds of the telephone being shifted, the door being closed, the scraping of a chair.

"Yes?"

"I want to sell it all."

Another silence. She could feel Alexandre's breathing, which she knew so well, in which she'd lost herself. She could hear it distinctly: excitement. His eyes must be shining at the gift being offered to him. Paradise. All of it.

"What are you talking about?"

"Stop playing dumb. Émilienne told me everything."

"We had an agreement, she and I," he said, defensively.

Blanche used her most resigned tone.

"I want to sell everything. Not just the pond. The rest of it, too."

He coughed. She held the receiver away from her ear.

"I'm ready, and Émilienne is too, to sell you the land near the road," she continued.

The ease with which she lied was astonishing even to her. There was dead silence on the line. Blanche thought he had hung up.

"Alexandre, are you there?"

"Yes."

The voice of a little boy.

"Come to Paradise day after tomorrow, and we'll talk about it some more."

He laughed nervously.

"What's the catch? Louis will be lying in wait to beat me to a pulp, is that it?"

"Louis is gone."

Blanche didn't need to be in the same room to see Alexandre's face changing under the influence of all the information he'd just been given, impossible to untangle.

"Why would you do that?"

Blanche took a deep breath.

"Louis is gone, Émilienne's very old, and"—she hesitated for a few seconds—"your presence is too strong here. I'm selling it all. I can't keep up the farm by myself. Either you come tomorrow, or I'll call another agency."

She hung up the phone. Behind her, in the vestibule, Émilienne watched her desolately.

"I hope you know what you're doing."

Breathing hard, she left the room with difficulty. The door creaked in the late afternoon breeze, and Blanche, one last time, saw Alexandre, in front of his wife and son, soiling her with shame.

T he colors of life drained out of Blanche. She walked through the house, tired of repeating the same movements every morning. Her hair, drier than hay, was knotted into a hard little bun on top of her head like a tightly wound ball of wool. The pulled-back style emphasized her once-triumphant face, the bones now standing out in sharp relief around her eyes and mouth and ears. Nothing was left of that face, distorted by hunger and the desire for vengeance, but the green of her eyes, now pale and cold, focused solely on the approaching moment, when Blanche would marshal all the force of her rage.

The cows.

The barn. The chickens.

Émilienne. Breakfast.

Blanche took a shower at midday. In the bathroom, which she hadn't visited in days, the mirror above the sink showed her the image of her own ravaged face. Rapidly, the hot steam obscured what was left of her body, blurring her life, marking her skin with painful red welts. She could hardly make out the contours of her own silhouette in this mirror in which, on rare occasions, she had once enjoyed looking at herself naked, admiring herself, thinking that these buttocks, this belly button, these breasts were pleasing to Alexandre.

At lunch, she drained a large glass of milk and cut a tomato into thin slices. She did the dishes and dried the plates and the silverware and the big platter with a clean dishcloth. Hunched in her chair, Émilienne watched this skeleton rattling around in her kitchen, applying frail joints to the activities of everyday life, in which every movement had become an ordeal.

Blanche went to Gabriel's house, where he told her he had found a job at the elementary school. He would be overseeing the study hall for older children for an hour and a half every day and possibly in the mornings, too, before school. Blanche congratulated him. He wanted to hug her, but she frightened him, so self-assured in this vanishing body. He confined himself to a soft, sad *goodbye* and she continued on her way to the village, walking alone, her back held very straight.

She sat down on the terrace. Aurore brought her a beer without waiting for her order. They exchanged a few pleasantries about this and that, customers, and business, and the money coming in and the money going out, and the weather, which never turns out how the forecast predicts. Blanche listened without hearing. She had already left Le Marché, the family, Paradise, sinking into the chasms inside her, focused on what was to come, obsessed by the violence that lay in each of her movements, each of her words.

After a long quarter of an hour, the Émards' daughter left the rickety table and went back home.

The sky was a steely white that hurt the eyes. Blanche wondered if her father, as he roamed through Paradise, had thought about what his children might grow up to be, if he'd ever imagined that those photos and diagrams and the notes in his beautiful, old-fashioned handwriting would turn out to be his ultimate legacy. That love for the land that had disappeared in an accident as foolish as those felt-tip pen sketches.

Everything was perfectly in place. Now she could see herself reflected in the eyes of others: a dead woman. Blanche drew in a deep breath as a voice from the past rose up in her, repeating to that fleshless, yet living reflection: *Never hurt anyone smaller than you. Or you'll suffer much worse in return.*

É milienne sat reading in her usual place in the dining room. Alexandre knocked on the door. She got up very slowly, made her way to the front hall, turned the knob.

He backed up, as surprised as she was.

"Is Blanche here?"

"She should be back any minute. You can come in and wait," Émilienne said to him absently.

Alexandre took another step backward and then hesitated, caught between what politeness required of him and his impatience to tour the property.

"I think I'll walk a bit, if you don't mind."

"Make yourself at home. If you want to go out to the pond, go past the pigpen and take the path down; it's the best way."

Alexandre looked where she was pointing, in the direction of a narrow passage next to the henhouse.

He crossed the yard, his steps tense. As he got further away from the porch, ducks and chickens surrounded him. His car was parked off the main road, in the little hollow that led to the farm. Sunlight flickered on the ground through the tall trees bordering the chicken coop. Alexandre's shadow stretched out in front of him. He walked more quickly, pursued by his memories. Something didn't feel right; the place seemed so quiet, so still. The gaggle of poultry that had escorted him to this point now turned around and went back to scratching and pecking. The path to the pigpen was well marked, its edges neatly trimmed. Insects hummed in the undergrowth. He was seized with the sudden desire to go that way, all the way to the far end of the property, as if to assess the extent of it.

Approaching the wide earthen circle ringed by a low fence, Alexandre froze. The pigs squealed, their attention drawn by his arrival. The young man leaned over the fence. The pen was shallow, broad, and clean. The shady part of it, where Louis normally emptied the scrap pail, was bathed in coolness by the tall oaks.

The pigs were grunting more and more loudly now. He remembered that day in the bedroom upstairs, when they'd made love for the first time while one of the beasts was slaughtered outside. He remembered its horrible cry, so long, so deep, so human. A shiver ran through him. The quiet of the farm clashed with the pigs' frenzy. They were now butting hard against the fence, ramming into it with all their weight. Frightened, Alexandre took a step back. The sound of leaves crunching made him jump. Someone was there, behind him.

Alexandre whirled around. The path was empty, its dry grass waving gently in the breeze. Only the faint, far-off noise of the chickens disturbed the silence.

"Is someone there?"

An answering moo from somewhere in the distance. A shudder of remembrance ran down his spine, the childhood memory of cows' eyes mocking his fear. Louis had left Paradise; Émilienne was barely hanging on, and Blanche, Blanche—he murmured her name, rubbing his temples to dispel his anxiety and collect his wits—Blanche was about to make him a rich man. Alexandre leaned his elbows on the gate. His pounding heart calmed at the thought of the contract he would be signing in less than an hour. Chin lifted, eyes closed, he savored the moment. These were his last few minutes as a poor man, a subservient employee, a hard-working husband and father. This evening, this afternoon, he would be a landowner.

Before he could turn, he felt something shove him against the wooden gate. The undone latch gave way and Alexandre toppled with the full force of his tall body, the body of an adult, so confident and soon to be rich, into the pen. The pigs rushed toward him, drawn by his scent, by the sudden movement. He sprawled in the shallow pit, his left ankle twisted at an odd angle, his hands fouled with dirt and liquid manure. Stunned, he tried to pull himself up on his forearms. A heavy mass struck him in the gut, spinning him back around, his leg now dragging uselessly behind him. The pigs surrounded him. He began screaming in terror. The pigs, which Blanche hadn't fed in two weeks, recoiled for a moment and then charged, tearing at the clothing, the skin, the guts of this scarecrow that had been suddenly thrown to them. Alexandre screamed for as long as he still could, his body being ripped apart, a prisoner of the voracious animals, and in the midst of his screaming, he saw Blanche's face, gaunt, emaciated, above the gate.

No one came. Émilienne was old. Louis wasn't here. No one came, except the pigs, clustering around him, famished, thrilled by this unexpected offering that had fallen from the sky. Alexandre let out one last scream and lost consciousness, the pigs' frenzied mouths shredding and tearing again and again at his beautiful body, his charming face. A large brownish pool spread along the dirt floor of the pen until it licked at the boards of the fence. As the body stopped quivering beneath the snouts dripping with blood and viscera, Blanche turned away from the gate of the pen and ran, her limbs flailing crazily, like a marionette shocked by an electric current, back to the house.

Sapped of what little strength remained to her, crushed by her own madness, she collapsed in the vestibule, grief and vengeance and savagery battling within her. Her love had died in Paradise, as all great hopes do.

They recovered Alexandre's body, or what was left of it. The pigs were destroyed, one after the other. Blanche, dazed, answered the questions that were fired at her two, three, four times: *at what time, where were you, how long has it been since you ate a proper meal, where is your farmhand, what was your relationship to the deceased.* At such-and-such o'clock, she said, I was in this place, I haven't eaten in a very long time, Louis is on vacation, but I don't know where, Alexandre and I used to be boyfriend and girlfriend, and then lovers, and then he left me. She told the truth, always the truth, and, faced with this young woman on whom life had turned its back, they looked away. She was hard to look at, truly. Eaten up by death.

One more corpse in Paradise; one more death added to the pile. The Émard charnel house's toll was increasing; it was impossible to think about anything else when you set foot in the yard: another death. Who will be next? Will they keep living here? Impossible to stay under a roof sheltering more ghosts than living people. Death in Paradise.

Aurore and Louis were summoned to the police station the day after the tragedy. The previous afternoon, at three o'clock, Gabriel had been on his way to the elementary school for one last interview; he'd been seen walking toward the village. Aurore had been working at the bar. As for Louis, on whom the majority of suspicion fell, he had been spotted in the city. He had spent his two weeks' vacation there, presenting himself at Alexandre's real estate office as a potential buyer. He'd been warmly welcomed, no one suspecting his true identity. Rarely venturing beyond the boundaries of Paradise, Louis was a stranger wherever he went.

The boss had greeted him obsequiously, and Louis had spent two weeks insisting that he accompany him to visit houses and apartments; then, one day, late in the afternoon, Louis had suggested that they go for a beer together; they deserved it, after all those visits. Calmly, Louis had grilled the man; he was a nice fellow, a bit money-hungry, but a good egg. It hadn't been difficult; he was a businessman, talking the same way he breathed, easily and loudly. Louis had mentioned that he thought he might know one of the employees whose picture he'd seen at the office. "Alexandre!" the man had laughed. "Ah, yes, our young newlywed!" And he'd gone on at length about Alexandre's honeymoon in New Zealand with his wife, and how he'd scored a big commission off a certain Doctor Neyrie when he'd gotten back. Alexandre had gloated about the deal for weeks, but business was bad, and the boss had almost fired him, "Last in, first out; I'm sure you understand." Alexandre had begged for another chance; he had an idea, a brilliant one, to buy up farmland in areas that were soon to be urbanized and resell it as buildable lots. What a fine young man Alexandre was; what a bright mind. Louis nodded, drinking more than was wise, repeating, "We're all looking for a fellow like that. When you find one, you don't let him get away."

The summer finally drew to an end with the arrival of newborn calves and scarlet leaves. Blanche was presiding over lunch on this Sunday in late August for the first time, Émilienne having yielded her place at the head of the table. Next to the Émards' daughter sat Louis, making sure her plate was never empty, that the silverware didn't fall and hit the muzzle of the dog, lying at Blanche's feet. She kept feeding the animal bits of chicken skin, feeling its rough tongue and smooth teeth against her fingers. Soon, the surface of Sombre-Étang would be covered with wide, round water lilies, the thick hedges trimmed back for the winter. Louis would cut down the chestnut trees ahead of the first frost, as always; Blanche insisted that it was the best wood for heating. She repeated the same actions every day, said the same things. Whenever her napkin fell on the ground, Louis picked it up for her, and she always chided him, "Why are you crouching down like that? You're not a dog." He would straighten up, setting the napkin on the table, or the dishcloth on the rim of the sink. Blanche would murmur again, and he never responded.

Aurore and Gabriel had come earlier than usual on this particular Sunday, helping Louis in the kitchen, the queen outside, calling out orders every now and then without getting up. They bustled around, and she believed she was directing them, pointing to the barn, the house, the chicken coop, Louis nodding. Reassured, she sat back in her chair, shoulders jutting out on either side of her thin, pale neck. When she wanted anything, she tapped twice on the table with her first and middle fingers, and the farmhand would fetch her a dish, or the salt, or a pitcher. Just before noon, Louis had set out the silverware and smoothed the tablecloth embroidered with the Émard family's initials in the shade of the red oak, the table held steady by wedges. The tree's leaves drooped in the summer heat. Blanche had to wipe sweat from her forehead whenever she left her chair or stretched an arm over the plates. Gabriel lolled in his chair, digesting the chicken he had carved. His fingers left brownish smudges on the tablecloth. Even before Blanche could get annoyed, Louis was soothing her, "Those things don't matter, Blanche. It doesn't matter."

"We're having a baby."

Aurore shivered. There, Gabriel had said it. They had agonized over the right day, the right place, the right time to break the news. Everyone at the table registered shock, Blanche staring at the porch steps, palms pressed flat against the sky-blue summer dress that draped her body like a shroud. She sat unmoving, mouth open, silent.

"Blanche? It's wonderful, they're going to have a baby!"

Slowly she turned her head to look at Louis; between the hollow, pale cheeks shaded gray in places from lack of sleep, her lips twitched. Aurore huddled against Gabriel. It was as if Blanche had left her body, as if her spirit was roaming somewhere outside her, indifferent to the trouble it was causing. The Émards' daughter murmured, dry-eyed:

"Let's go and tell Alexandre; he'll be happy to hear it."

Mechanically, she slipped a hand into her pocket, pulling out three flower stems withered from the heat, the same kind of flowers that grow along the asphalt road all year round, a wild little bouquet that she would place, as she did every day, in the pigpen. Then, wobbling on her bony legs, she rose from her chair and flung her arms wide in a shambling movement that seemed as if it might rip her body open from throat to belly button. Head thrown back, she embraced this yard, this chicken coop, this house, these distant meadows, this barn, and this Sombre-Étang, broken by the mad love she had for Paradise.

ACKNOWLEDGEMENTS

The author is deeply grateful to Marie Nimier
and Sylvie Pereira for their editorial advice.